Accla

"This is a very suspenseful story and I'm looking forward to the next book in this series."—Ginny, Amazon reviewer

"I was impressed with the suspense in this book as well as the romance. Great storyline. Morality issues were great. An overall great read."—Kindle customer

"Absolutely loved it. Fast paced and kept me guessing concerning the outcome. I highly recommend it to all who like a good mystery or suspense."—Linda Reville

"Very well written, with interwoven stories and well developed characters"—Mary L. Sarrault

Other books by JL Crosswhite

Hometown Heroes series
Promise Me, prequel novella
Protective Custody, book 1
Flash Point, book 2
Special Assignment, book 3

The Route Home series, writing as Jennifer Crosswhite
Be Mine, prequel novella
Coming Home, book 1
The Road Home, book 2

Contemporary romance, writing as Jennifer Crosswhite
The Inn at Cherry Blossom Lane

Devotional, writing as Jennifer Crosswhite
Worthy to Write: Blank pages tying your stomach in knots? 30 prayers to tackle that fear!

PROMISE ME

HOMETOWN HEROES
BOOK 0

Blessings!
Jennifer

JL CROSSWHITE

Copyright

Published by Tandem Services Press
Post Office Box 220
Yucaipa, California
www.TandemServicesInk.com

ISBN 978-0-9995357-0-7 print
ISBN 978-0-9995357-1-4 ebook

Cover photo credit: Depositphoto

Chapter One

Orange County, California

THE FOG WAS CALLING. CAIT Bellamy lifted her digital SLR camera off the passenger seat of her Jetta. No point in bringing the whole camera bag when she wouldn't use more than the zoom lens already attached. She liked the challenge provided by having only one lens with her. Gravel crunched under her Keds as she stepped out into the parking lot, shutting and locking her car before tucking the keys in her pocket.

Slinging her camera over her shoulder—and freeing her long, blonde hair from under the strap—she passed the Samashima farm store, busy even though it was Valentine's Day. Maybe people were hoping to make last-minute chocolate-covered strawberries from the early producers. Those strawberries weren't nearly as sweet as the later spring ones would be.

She waved at her boss Alani through the window and kept going. Since it was Sunday and almost two o'clock, Alani would be closing soon. They kept short hours on Sunday so everyone who wanted to had a chance to go to church. She loved the Samashimas and how they treated all their workers like family, just as their parents before them had.

Fog hung like a damp blanket over the emerald rows that stretched back toward the foothills. The smell of damp earth and mulch enveloped her, causing her shoulders to ease down. As she headed past the main building where her office was, she noted all the lights were off. The Samashimas kept work minimal on Sundays, an aberration in this modern world. But they believed in the importance of rest, regardless of your religious beliefs, as part of the natural order of things, that working seven days a week would make you less productive, not more.

Cait wasn't so sure. She didn't work here on Sundays, but she couldn't remember the last Sunday she wasn't working on restoring her farmhouse, even when she sang in the choir at church for three services. But the house was another problem she was escaping today.

She declined an invitation to go out to lunch with other singles from church, sort of an anti-Valentine's Day thing. But she was at a frustrating point with her house renovation, and she needed a break.

It wasn't that she was anti-Valentine's Day; she had good memories of it with her Grandma. They'd always make a special dessert. When she was eleven, they'd made a strawberry soufflé. Her mouth watered even now thinking of it. She had considered making something today, but with no one to share it with, she'd be eating dessert all week.

She'd learned to enjoy her own company from years of eating microwave dinners in front of the TV while her parents were out. Once Grandma had taught her to cook, her meals improved. But cooking was always better when done for more than one person. Maybe she should have invited the singles over to her house. But with as much of it in shambles as it was, it probably wasn't safe.

And now she was thinking far too much for a day where she was supposed to escape with her camera.

Far enough into the fields, she stopped and looked around. The fog created lovely tendrils of mist. The diffused sun laid a lovely, soft light on the young strawberry plants. Cait composed the image in her mind before lifting her camera. She took some readings, refined her settings, and then began shooting. After a few shots, she checked the display on the back of her camera. Satisfied, she let her work absorb her, pushing aside, for now, everything else that threatened to consume her.

Grayson Kendall slid the creeper out from under the '66 Mustang, wiping his hands on a rag. "Try that, Dad."

Dad cranked the key and, after a bit of sputtering, the old girl turned over and began running like a champ.

Grayson leaned under the hood and made some adjustments before closing it. "I think that'll do it."

Dad climbed out of the car and grinned. "Glad you figured it out. Just in time for me to take your mother for a little Valentine's Day spin." He tapped the roof.

"It's a little foggy to head out to the beach." Grayson picked up tools and began returning them to their places. He was glad his folks were happy. Maybe that'd be him too. Someday.

"Ah, we have our places you know nothing of. We've had a few years' practice, you know." Dad picked up the last tool, placed it in the drawer and pushed it shut.

"I know. Go have a good time."

"We will. I appreciate your help, son." Dad paused. "You have any plans?"

Grayson didn't miss the significance of the pause. That was about as prying as Dad got. "Oh yeah. Pizza and a movie and my couch." The pizza sounded good, and he'd probably have a movie playing in the background, but he'd be working on a new land development proposal he was trying to pull together. He had to get moving on it before someone else grabbed it, but he never seemed to have time with his other work. His folks thought he worked too hard as it was, even though they didn't quite understand what a real estate attorney did all day.

He opened the door to the house before this conversation could go any further. "I'm giving Mom a hug goodbye, and then I'll be out of here." Before Mom could start in on him too.

Cait leaned back and stretched. She'd been in some awkward positions getting the shots she wanted. Luckily, there was no one out here to witness her contortions. She couldn't wait to upload her photos to her monitor and see how they looked. She glanced at her phone. Whoa! She'd been out here for hours, much longer than she'd thought. Well, time did that when she was absorbed with something she enjoyed. It happened often when she was working on a house project.

Her stomach growled. Time to eat anyway. She headed back.

An odd sound floated across the field. Fog could carry sound in weird ways, but this almost sounded like running water. But there was no running water anywhere out in the fields. Back in the day, there used to be irrigation ditches, but now everything was done through drip irrigation.

In the barn area, there were pumps and faucets, but there was no way she should be able to hear any water from there out here. Plus, being Sunday, no one would be in the barn.

She stopped. Footsteps?

Maybe she was hearing things. Nope. Definitely water.

She hopped over rows of plants and headed to the access road where she could make better time. Orienting toward the sound of the water, she picked up her pace, but the fog made it more difficult to discern the direction of the sound. Closer now, it was definitely water.

A shape moved in and out of the fog. Someone else was here. Mario? None of this made any sense.

The fog parted, and she spied the irrigation controls. Water was spewing out all over the ground. One of them must have broken. She reached for her phone.

A man darted from behind one of the storage sheds, looked right at her, and froze. Tall, blond, broad shoulders. If he had a plaid shirt, he would look like a lumberjack.

Barely thinking, she brought up her camera and snapped off a bunch of shots. No idea if the settings were right or if she'd get anything usable.

The man's face reddened, and he ran toward the parking lot.

Shaking, she lowered the camera and fumbled for her phone. She touched the screen at Mario's number and gave him a brief rundown. As she talked, she jogged toward the irrigation controls. Water flooded in every direction, creating a rapidly enlarging pond drowning the nearby strawberry plants. Her shoes immediately soaked through. "It looks like the lines were ripped off and the valves opened. I can try to shut them off."

"Do what you can." Mario's voice came through the phone.

She looked closer at the pipes coming out of the ground. "Scratch that. I won't be able to shut them off. Everything's been smashed open."

Mario swore. "I'll be out there right away. I'll call Makoa on the way. You call the police."

Cait stared at the disconnected phone. The police? Her boss, yes, he should know, and she was glad Mario was calling him and she didn't have to. The severity of what she was looking at stunned her. Water lapped her ankles. If they couldn't get this under control, they stood to lose a good part of their strawberry crop before it even got off the ground.

Gingerly stepping out of the water, she headed back to her car. She'd call the police and wait there for them since there was nothing she could do to stop the flow of water. Her stomach churned.

Rounding the farm store, she saw her lonely car in the parking lot. But it looked odd. It sat lower than normal. And she hadn't left the windows down.

A sick feeling threatened to overwhelm her. Her tires had been slashed and her windows smashed out. Hands shaking, she dialed 911.

Chapter Two

Google Maps told Grayson he had arrived at his destination. He wasn't so sure. He looked at the address on the house and compared it to what he had. Yep, this was it. An old farmhouse on the edge of a new development. Somehow it had managed not to be torn down. But it was clearly a work in progress. Peeling paint and a sagging front porch stood in contrast to the blooming front yard where camellias stood sentry on each side of the porch stairs. Purple verbena lined the front beds dotted with orange California poppies while the pink tulip tree in the front yard was in full bloom.

Maybe Cait lived with a relative. Bernie hadn't said anything about it when he had called and asked if Grayson could give her a ride to choir practice. He had jumped at the chance and hadn't asked for details.

Before Bernie had called, Grayson had planned on skipping rehearsal because he needed to put more time in on his real estate deal. Though as yet unseen, he felt his competition breathing down his neck. The clock was ticking, and he needed every minute.

And if it had been anyone but Cait, he would have put Bernie off. Grayson had had his eye on Cait ever since he joined the choir last fall. During the marathon Christmas season, he had managed to sit by her in the green room one night and they talked through several services. He had enjoyed her company and wanted to get to know her better. But since then, he hadn't had the opportunity to get her alone to ask her out. So this seemed like a perfect opportunity to spend some time with her, if only for the short car ride to and from church.

He got out of his car and headed up the warped porch steps to the front door, wiping his hands on his jeans before he twisted the old-fashioned doorbell. Why did it feel like a date?

The door swung open almost immediately, and Cait's bright smile appeared through the old wooden screen door. She pushed it open. "Hi! Come on in. I just have to grab my music folder."

"Hey, this is a great place. I didn't know any farmhouses had escaped development." He looked around the small entry way. Scuffed wood floors led to the back of the house. Stairs in front of him led upstairs. The newel post was solid wood and beautifully carved. The banister looked like it was in the process of being stripped of paint. The house was a grand old lady that just needed a bit of sprucing up.

Cait lifted a folder off a console table in the hall and grabbed her purse. "It barely did. I bought it from the city for back taxes after the owner died. The developer that built the homes in the rest of the neighborhood offered me a lot of money for it. If I was smart, I probably should have taken him up on it. But I just couldn't see this place torn down."

He reached out and rubbed the newel post. "This is fantastic. You just don't see craftsmanship like this anymore."

Cait tilted her head. "If you're interested sometime, I'll give you a tour. But it'll take more time than we have right now."

"I'll take you up on that." He turned and opened the front door for her then waited while she locked up. Taking a few quick steps, he opened her car door for her.

"Thanks." She slid gracefully into his low-slung Dodge Charger.

He closed the door once she was settled and hustled around to his side. This was not a date, though it sure felt like one.

Once they were on the road headed toward church, he glanced at her. "So what happened to your car? Bernie didn't say."

Cait blew out a long breath.

"That bad, huh?"

"Complicated. The short answer is someone slashed all the tires and smashed out the windows Sunday. Then the rental car wouldn't start when I tried to leave work today. My boss gave me a ride home." She tugged a lock of hair over her shoulder.

"Random vandalism? Or is there more to it than that?"

"It happened at work. I'm the marketing director for Samashima Farms, and I was out there taking pictures. Someone had destroyed the irrigation pipes, damaging our strawberry crop. I saw a guy run off. And I called the police, but they aren't sure what's going on."

He wanted to know more, but by the time he got his thoughts in order they were pulling into the church parking lot. Was Cait in danger? Did this guy she saw know who she was?

He hustled around the car and got her door open before she had gathered her purse and music folder. He resisted the urge to reach for her hand as they walked into the church together. Soon they were surrounded by fellow choir members. He reached out and touched Cait's arm.

Her gaze met his, and she gave him a warm smile.

He almost forgot what he was going to say. "I'll meet you after practice, okay?"

She nodded. "Thank you."

"My pleasure." And it absolutely was. He knew one thing: as much as that real estate deal was calling for his attention, giving Cait a ride was the best choice he could have made. And he was going to milk it for all it was worth.

"So, I'll see you around 7:30 tomorrow?" Heather McAlistair said, just as Grayson joined them. Cait's nerve endings went on high alert around him. With his dark hair, blue eyes, and dimples, Grayson had always been attractive to Cait. Getting to spend some time with him, short as it was, confirmed what she'd always known about him: that he was a genuinely nice guy. A rare commodity these days.

"That'd be great. Thanks. I'll buy you coffee." Cait slung her purse over her shoulder, trying to appear casual.

"Anything for coffee." Heather waved and left the choir room.

"Ready to go?" Grayson said to Cait, touching her arm and creating a shock that raced through her whole body.

"Yep." She hoped her voice sounded casual and even.

They walked toward the parking lot. "Is Heather giving you a ride to work tomorrow?"

"Yes, I'll get the rental company to bring me a new car at work. It never fails when I'm running around late that stuff like this happens. This week has been one disaster after another." Brilliant. Any guy would be attracted to a disaster magnet.

"It always seems to happen that way, doesn't it?" Grayson opened the car door for her.

She murmured her thanks and slid into the Dodge Charger, the leather seats wrapping around her. Even though she drove a sporty Jetta, she had a thing for muscle cars, especially the retro ones from the 60s and 70s. But this newer model was pretty nice too.

Grayson pulled out of the parking lot, and she couldn't figure out what to say. Should she comment on his car or would that sound like some bubbly girl trying to flatter him? The silence stretched out awkwardly. She was wasting this time with him. She wracked her brain but could come up with nothing. Big old blank slate.

He glanced over at her. "So tell me the whole story about your car now that we're not pressed for time."

Her shoulders relaxed. This she could do. She told him about taking pictures, hearing the water, seeing the man run off—"Oh, wow! I just remembered." She covered her mouth with her hand. With all the activity about the busted pipes and her car, she completely forgot.

She turned to Grayson. "I have a picture of the guy on my camera."

Grayson leaned over the back of Cait's chair as she fiddled with her computer. Her hair smelled faintly sweet and tropical. Like mangoes. He hoped his sniffing wasn't obvious.

"Here it is." A series of photos flashed on her large monitor, arranging themselves as thumbnails in a grid as they loaded from her flash card. She clicked on one to enlarge it to fill the whole screen. A green strawberry leaf dotted with dew and a delicate white flower appeared. Something ordinary turned lovely by an unusual perspective.

She clicked through a few more—too quickly for him to study them—before she slowed. Fog covered most of the screen with damp ground at the bottom. And a shadowy figure. She clicked again though the next few photos as the figure emerged and receded. Finally, she stopped. "There."

It wasn't the clearest picture, but it was as good as those he'd seen from surveillance cameras. What did it all mean?

Cait dug through her desk drawer and pulled out a business card. "Here it is. Detective Kyle Taylor, Laguna Vista PD. I need to call him tomorrow and tell him about this." She clicked a few more times before shutting her computer down. She put the flash card in a small case and stacked it on top of the detective's card.

He leaned back in his chair. "Who do you think that is?"

Cait stood. "Do you want some coffee? I can make decaf."

He smiled. That was the best offer he'd had all night. "Sounds great." He followed her out of the living room, where her desk was set up in a corner, through the dining room.

She skirted around the edge of the room. "Watch your step." She pointed to a sheet of plywood laying on the dining room floor.

He followed her footsteps. "What's the deal with that?"

She grimaced. "The floorboards are rotten. You might end up in the root cellar. Yet something else on my never-ending to-do list."

He caught a glimpse of her overwhelming burden. It seemed nearly impossible that she could rehab this house by herself. Wait. "Root cellar? That's pretty rare around here."

"It's creepy is what it is. I think it was mostly used for storing canning jars. Spiders and bugs love it. I stay out of it." She shivered and then stepped through the doorway into the kitchen.

"Wow!" In contrast to the clearly in-progress dining and living rooms, the kitchen was beautifully remodeled. Soapstone countertops, apron-front farmhouse sink, beadboard cupboards. Classic subway tile backsplash. Stainless steel appliances and a commercial-type range. "This is gorgeous."

"Thanks." She started the coffee in a bright red Keurig. "Cream? Sugar?"

"Cream, thanks."

"This was my second project. My first was the master bath. I figured if I had a bathroom and a kitchen, I could handle going without a lot of other things." She handed him his mug of coffee.

"Did you do the work yourself?" He couldn't quite wrap his mind around petite Cait doing the heavy lifting a remodel like this would require.

"A lot of it. I contracted out the plumbing and electric. But

I refinished and rearranged all the cabinets myself, calling in a few favors when I needed some muscle. I tiled the backsplash. Got the soapstone countertops from another old house and had them resurfaced." She leaned against the island—shoulders relaxed and a smile soft around her lips—sipping from her mug.

He shook his head, amazed. "That is really something. My dad and I restore old cars, so I know a bit about what you're talking about, but this is a huge project."

She tilted her head. "I'll show you the rest of the house."

Huh. So the subject of what happened at the farm was tabled for now. He'd follow her lead, but he wasn't leaving here tonight without a better sense of the danger she was in.

Cait wasn't sure what made her decide to show Grayson her house—all of it, the completed parts and the works in progress. She'd shown it to so few people. Most thought she was crazy for attempting a project this ambitious. But he seemed so interested and complimentary of the work she had done. Plus, she liked having him around. It was a work night, so she knew he wouldn't be able to stay much longer, but talking about her house was better than thinking about what happened at the farm, and what that could mean for her.

They were back in the kitchen, perched on barstools.

"Too bad it's too dark or I'd show you my gardens." She gestured toward a glass door that led to the backyard. "They actually look pretty good."

"You garden too? I'll have to come back another time and see them."

"You can blame my grandma." She laughed. "I spent most of my days after school at her house learning how to garden, cook, sew, fix things." She hugged her arms across her middle. "Makes me feel close to her, I guess."

Grayson nodded. "I can understand that. I've worked with my dad on cars since I was old enough to hand him tools. My older brother, Daniel, wasn't interested so it was something Dad and I could do together." He set his mug down. "About that guy in the picture. Do you know who he is?"

She shook her head. "No. I've been thinking about it ever since. It seems like the work of a disgruntled employee who wanted to get back at us. But the Samashimas treat everyone so well, and they haven't let go of anyone lately. We've actually been expanding. A lot of restaurants want to carry our produce. We grow more than just strawberries. And the farm store is always busy, so we've hired more help for that."

"If you weren't there, and he succeeded in flooding the whole area, what would have happened?"

This was exactly where she didn't want to go. The coffee soured in her stomach. "It would have been really bad. We could have lost a good portion of our strawberry crop. That would have cost us commercial and retail customers. Probably some restaurants. We would have to lay off people." She met his gaze. "And I would take a huge cut in pay since most of my salary is commission off commercial and restaurant sales."

He didn't say anything, just stared into his coffee mug. When he looked up at her, his blue eyes had darkened. "Do you feel safe staying here?"

Chapter Three

Ensconced in her office at the farm, Cait hung up the phone. Detective Taylor was on his way over. She turned his card over in her fingers thinking about what Grayson had asked her last night. Other than the creepy root cellar, she'd never felt unsafe in her own house. She'd been alone so much growing up that empty houses didn't bother her.

But she was uneasy. Was that from the farm vandalism or something else? Working for a farm meant her job security was based on the whims of the weather, pests, market, and a whole lot of other things she couldn't control. She couldn't see the damaged area from her office window, and she had specifically avoided it the last few days. It was bad enough to see the broken glass from her car windows in the parking lot until Mario had someone sweep it up.

This was a one-time thing. It had to be. None of it made any sense. But there couldn't be any more to it because she couldn't lose any accounts. In fact, she needed at least two more to earn enough money to bring the rest of the electrical in her house up to code. She couldn't do anything else until that happened. And she was out of money.

At the knock on her doorframe, she turned from her mindless gazing at the computer. A tall man with broad shoulders and close-cut sandy blond hair filled the doorway.

She stood from her seat, extending her hand, "Detective Taylor, I presume."

He shook it. "And you must be Cait Bellamy." He glanced at the coffee cup on her desk, courtesy of her pit stop with Heather this morning as payment for bringing Cait to work. "I spend way too much time at the Jitter Bug. Great coffee and great desserts. That's hard to beat."

She laughed. "I know. It's ridiculously tempting." She turned her monitor so he could see it better. "Here are the photos I got. They aren't the greatest, but maybe they'll be of some help."

His gray eyes studied the monitor, not saying much other than having her switch between the photos. "Can you print me copies and email the full-size files to me? I'll see if our guys can do anything to clean these up."

"Sure." She sent the files to print. Swallowing, she asked, "Do you have any more information on who might have done this? Or why?"

He shook his head. "Nothing yet, but we have a few leads we're pursuing."

She pulled the photos off the printer tray and handed them to him.

"Thanks for these. I'll let you know if anything comes of this." He left her office.

After emailing him the files, she leaned back in her chair. Work was elusive today. She poked around the farm's social media sites, but she couldn't do justice to analyzing any metrics.

She thought about sitting in her kitchen with Grayson, drinking coffee last night. A warmth curled through her stomach. She had enjoyed it. When would she see him again? He had said he wanted to view her garden, but maybe he was just being nice. He'd also looked straight into her eyes when he'd told her to call him for any reason. He'd grabbed her cell phone and punched his number in.

Turning back to her computer, she pulled up her house project spreadsheet from Google Drive. Was there anything else she could work on until the electrical was done? Had she missed something?

Nope. Other than the kitchen, which had already been gutted and rewired, everything in the house had the potential to be disturbed by running new wires for fixtures and outlets.

She could work on patching the dining room floor, but the idea of going into the root cellar underneath it gave her the willies. She'd have to see who she could recruit to help her. Grayson's face flashed through her mind, but she immediately dismissed it. She couldn't possibly ask him. She hadn't known him long enough to ask for such a big favor.

In the meantime, it looked like her garden and landscaping was going to get a lot of attention.

As for Grayson, if she didn't run into him at church on Sunday, she would see him at choir practice. That was going to have to be good enough for now.

Or so she told herself.

Grayson stepped into his office. A pile of papers had grown overnight, thanks to his too-efficient administrative assistant. He flipped through them. Contracts, legal descriptions, owners' rolls.

He plopped into his chair and blew out a breath. He really wanted to call Cait and see what the detective had said about those photos. Even though he'd told her to call him for anything, he knew she wouldn't. She was too self-possessed. Look at all she had done on that house by herself.

Still, who would target that farm? What could they possibly gain?

In his world, it would be land. It was all about land. So did someone want the farm? The land would be valuable as a development. And many farmers had sold out over the past decades just for that reason, choosing to take the certainty of the cash over the variability of farming.

Wondering… he logged into his computer and pulled up a map of the farm. With a little digging, he was able to find out who owned the land surrounding the farm. DiMarco Development owned a lot. No surprise. They were a big player in the area. One he hoped he could work with on the deal he was trying to put together himself.

He closed the tabs. He had plenty of work to do, even without the big deal. He had a client that owned some land that he wanted to develop but didn't know how. He had another client with land not too far away. If they could get the land connecting them, get the right developers involved, pull together some engineers and architects who were willing to invest their time and talents, as well as some financial backers, this could be huge. The payoff would be great for everyone involved.

And most of all, it would prove that his analytical mind was good for more than just reading through contracts and fine print. He could actually make deals. He could point to something physical and say, "I did that."

With a bit more research, he could put the finishing touches on his presentation and start going down the list of the people he needed to get on board.

Including his boss, who more than once had told him to forget it, that it would never work. Grayson had heard that before, but he had a few lost-cause projects under his belt to know enough to trust his instincts. Too bad his boss hadn't been impressed. So Grayson had no slack on his other work. The development had to be a side deal.

The pile of paperwork called to him, but he needed more

coffee before he could tackle it. And before he could change his mind, he punched up Cait's number. Lunch would be a good distraction and give him something to look forward to.

Cait's phone buzzed, and she jumped. Grayson's name appeared on the screen. She stared at it, hands shaking. It was almost as if she had conjured him up by her thoughts. But, no, he was really calling.

She fumbled to answer before it went to voice mail.

Grayson's voice, warm as sunshine, came through the phone. "So I know this is late notice and you probably already have plans, but since I figured you might still be stuck at work without a car, I wondered if you were up for lunch."

A thousand thoughts flooded her brain and begged for attention. She grabbed onto one of them to shove out her mouth. "Sure. I'd love to."

"Great! I'll see you in about 30 minutes. Think about where you want to go."

Still shaking, she dropped her phone on her desk. Suppressing a giggle, she fell back against her chair. This was ridiculous. It was just lunch, and she wasn't in high school crushing on the big football star.

But it did fan the flame of hope that he was interested in her, beyond just being a nice guy doing a good deed. She pulled out a mirror from her desk drawer and quickly checked her hair and makeup, thinking she was being completely ridiculous the whole time. Still, she continued.

Don't get your hopes up. There was a reason she kept to herself for the most part. People could be nice on the surface, but the moment you put any hope or trust in them, they would disappoint you. And she didn't want to be disappointed by Grayson.

Telling her butterflies to be realistic, she picked up the

phone. The rental car company still hadn't dropped off her new car. She had time for a quick call before Grayson got here. Not that she would get much done today anyway. A short conversation, and the car agency assured her they were sending someone out within the hour and they would leave the keys in the office if she wasn't there.

That taken care of, she grabbed her purse and headed outside. Might as well expend some nervous energy walking around the farm. She could head to the barn and see if any babies had been born since her last visit. Everybody loved pictures of the babies on social media. The hobby farm was a big hit with kids and grownups too. Most people weren't around farm animals anymore.

Watching where she stepped, she laughed as the chickens scattered before her, clucking their discontent with her disturbance. The goats were in their pen, climbing up the obstacles set in there for them and knocking each other off. The pregnant one was still rounded. No kid yet.

She imagined that's what having siblings must be like. As an only child, she'd always wished she'd had a brother or sister to keep her company when her folks were gone. But she did enjoy having Grandma's attention all to herself.

She walked through the open barn door, the smell of straw, manure, and animals strangely comforting. She checked the pens of the cows. No babies there either.

Conscious of going out to lunch, she avoided touching anything. But she could still look. She leaned over the railing of the last stall. Nope. Pulling back, her shirt tightened around her. What?

She searched for what was restraining her but couldn't see anything. Tugging, she heard a ripping sound just before she was freed. The lower flare of her tunic had gotten caught on a raised nail head hidden under the rail. A nice swatch of the fabric remained on the nail.

The shirt still covered her, but it was obvious a chunk was

missing. Normally, she'd just hide in her office the rest of the day, but Grayson was coming. Gah!

She hustled out of the barn, blinking at the sunlight. A beautiful day, no matter that it was February. She rearranged her purse to cover the worst of the tear. Maybe he wouldn't notice. Men never noticed what women were wearing, right?

Grayson forced himself to remember to eat as he sat with Cait on the patio of a local food court. Even though it was technically still winter, it felt like a beautiful, early summer day. That was California for you.

But as beautiful as the day was with a light breeze and puffy clouds skidding across the cadet blue sky, it didn't hold a candle to Cait. Even with the rip across the bottom of her shirt that she tried to hide with her purse.

"What did Detective Taylor say when he saw the photos?" Grayson shoved a bite into his mouth.

"Not much. He said he'd be in touch if they found anything." The wind lifted her pretty blonde hair, and he had to focus again.

"So no disgruntled employees. And if it's vandalism, it's an odd choice." Two pieces of information collided in Grayson's brain. He swallowed the rest of his food as he considered what he should say next. "I told you I was a real estate attorney, but I don't think I told you I specialize in commercial development. So naturally, my mind goes to land and who owns it."

Cait nodded and took a sip of her drink.

"I looked into who owned the land around Samashima Farms. It's an interesting mix of developers and only one other private owner. Do you know if there have been any offers to buy the farm lately?"

She waved the thought away. "There are always offers.

Some very good ones. But the farm has been in the family since after World War II when Makoa's grandfather got out of the Japanese internment camp at Manzanar. It's important to them that it stay in the family, more so than any financial offer."

He leaned forward. "So they wouldn't sell voluntarily. But what would force them to sell? That land is prime for commercial development. Nearly everything around it has been sold and developed."

Her eyes filled with wariness, confusion, and then understanding. She leaned forward. "Whoa. I hadn't thought about that. But wait, what that guy did, that wasn't enough to put them out of business. Not even close. But it could make things uncomfortable." Her gaze dropped.

"True. But maybe it was because you stopped him."

The color drained from her face, and she sagged in her chair. "So that's why he trashed my car."

"It's possible, yes. Or he wanted to make it look like more vandalism."

"What do you think he's going to do next?"

He shook his head. "I wish I knew. Has he given up because you scared him off, or was that just the first of other things he has planned?" He paused. "I do have one more question for you."

"What's that?"

"Who was the developer that wanted to buy your farmhouse?"

"DiMarco Development. Why do you ask?"

He pressed his lips together. "I'm not sure. But if there's even the remotest chance that you're a target, I want to have all the information I can get."

"What makes you think I am the target?" She wrapped her arms around her middle.

"I'm not sure that you are. But you do work for Samashima Farms, and it was your car he trashed. And you saw him."

She looked out across the parking lot, her brow furrowed.

He could kick himself. Now she was upset and worried. This was not the way he wanted to have lunch with her. Once again it seemed like his father was right; Grayson couldn't finish things well without some help.

Chapter Four

Cait had her routine. Every morning, steaming cup of tea in hand, she stepped into the garden behind her farmhouse. Walking between the raised beds, she touched the leaves, felt the soil, gauged their growth, looked for pests. She could nearly do it in her sleep.

It felt good and right to get back to it now that she had a working rental car and didn't need a ride to work.

Instead of tea, she had switched to coffee this morning. She needed it today after not sleeping well last night thinking about all that Grayson had told her at lunch. Was she a target? She couldn't see how. But she startled at every creak the old house made last night, even though they normally were as comforting and familiar as a favorite worn blanket.

He seemed apologetic and a bit regretful that he had told her his concerns. But she assured him that she was glad he had shared them. They were things she would not have thought of. It was kind of him to get involved. He didn't have to do anything, but he did. That touched her in a place she hadn't thought about in a long time.

Not to mention he had been too polite to mention the rip in her shirt even though it was difficult to hide.

He had dropped her back at the farm with a promise to get ahold of her over the weekend so he could come see her garden. That was great, but she wasn't going to hold her breath. Guys said things like that all the time. Still, Grayson seemed different. But it was early days yet.

She was used to her own company. An image flashed through her mind of when she would come home from school to an empty house that would gradually grow darker. She would make a frozen dinner and eat it by the light of the TV and put herself to bed. Sometimes she wondered if her parents even remembered they had a kid.

So someone who was new in her life would have to go a long way to prove that they wouldn't forget about her too.

Now what should she do with the information he had given her? The rosemary released its spicy scent as she ran her fingertips across it. She walked through her raised beds looking at her plants, pulling at a young weed here and there. She plucked a few ripe Meyer lemons and some Valencia oranges. She would need to give some away, she had so many. She peered over at her side yard. It could use some work. Maybe tomorrow. Weeding was one of the best ways she knew to mull something over.

But first, she needed to tell the Samashimas what Grayson had told her. Alani would be in the office this morning. Makoa would be out in the fields with the workers, but Alani would call him in. They at least need to know Grayson's suspicions. Even if they were unfounded. It was possible the Samashimas had information Cait didn't.

And she had to do one other thing in this week that had been unproductive in the extreme. She had to get more accounts.

Cait tossed her purse on the kitchen counter. She'd love to forget this week. Other than the time she had spent with Grayson, it was an utter wreck. She'd driven down to Laguna Beach to call on half a dozen restaurant managers who she had previously been in contact with who had indicated interest in Samashima Farm's Farm-to-Table restaurant produce supply program. Not one had bit, not even a nibble.

She kicked her shoes off and slipped on her gardening clogs. To top it off, her car still wasn't ready. There had been a delay in getting parts. She headed out to a small teak bench in the garden under the fruitless mulberry tree, the sunlight filtering through its branches swaying in the breeze, making shadows dance around her. She had spent a lot of time in her grandma's backyard laying under the tree, watching the shadows and sunlight play tag.

Her mind drifted back to a familiar memory, one where they were sitting in the backyard, trying to catch a breeze and get out of the hot kitchen where she'd been learning to bake.

"Promise me you won't forget to check on the cake." Grandma bent over to look Cait in the eye.

Cait nodded.

Grandma gave her a small smile and grasped Cait's chin. "Promise me you'll read your Bible every day. Promise me you'll check on the garden, even in the winter. Promise me you'll teach someone else all that I've taught you."

Cait nodded. "I promise." She'd do whatever Grandma said. She knew so much. But why was she being so serious today?

Now, Cait's eyes filled with tears. Looking back, Cait understood that Grandma had known Cait's parents were getting divorced. She wanted Cait focused on the good in her life and the things she knew how to do. Grandma had been a wise woman, something Cait appreciated more as she got older.

What would Grandma do with all of this? The job, the vandal, her house's electrical system. Grayson.

She'd pray, that's what she would do.

Cait took a deep breath and let it all out, asking God to

lift the weight that pushed her shoulders down with worry and to give her wisdom. Wiping her eyes, she took a final deep breath and headed inside. Once in the kitchen, she flipped on the TV to listen to the local news while she rummaged through the fridge.

The newscaster's voice came out of the TV. "Have you seen this man? The Laguna Vista Police Department released these images today of a man suspected of vandalizing Samashima Farms on Sunday."

Cait whipped around and caught the pictures she took flashing across the TV screen.

The newscaster spoke about the damage to the farm and asked viewers to call in if they had any information.

Slumping on the kitchen stool, Cait put her head in her hands. This was going to ruin her chance of getting any new accounts to sign up. What a perfect mess of a week.

Grayson hung up the phone and rubbed his hand across his face. That was the fifth voice mail he'd gotten. He glanced at the time. It was after five. No wonder no one was answering.

But was it more than that? No return emails or phone calls. He needed to get the key players to at least listen to his proposal, now that he'd finished it, or this project wasn't going to happen. And he was running out of time.

When he was poking around the land owners' rolls to see about Samashima Farms, he noticed that another key property had changed ownership. To DiMarco Development.

It wasn't surprising that DiMarco Development kept popping up. They were a big player and key to his project. But was it a coincidence that they had just bought land adjacent to Samashima Farms and were responsible for the development around Cait's farmhouse?

Probably. Besides, if anything shady was going on with

them, his whole development project would fall apart.

A cold chill shot through him. That couldn't happen. He couldn't even think about this project not coming together.

He leaned back in his chair. He needed to get out of the office, but he didn't particularly feel like heading home to his townhouse. He wished he had something like Cait's farmhouse to work on or another project car in his garage.

He could head over to his folks and get dinner out of it. Yep, that was a good plan.

Twenty minutes later, he walked through the front door of his folks' house. Smelled like meatloaf and mashed potatoes. His stomach rumbled.

"Hi, Mom." He hugged Mom around the waist and kissed her cheek. "Smells delicious. Hope you don't mind that I invited myself over."

"Of course not. There's always enough to go around. But you can set the table. Your brother is out back with your dad."

"Daniel's here?"

"Yes, he brought the most adorable little dog with him. He and your dad are playing with him in the backyard."

He looked out the dining room window. Daniel was throwing a ball to a small dog with a shaggy, coppery coat while Dad watched.

Grabbing the plates and silverware, he said, "So, did he get another dog?" He began setting the table, the routine familiar to him since he was a boy.

"No, that one belongs to his boss, but he's trying to get rid of it. He can tell you the whole story at dinner."

The slider opened, and Dad and Daniel came in.

"Go wash up and we'll eat," Mom called from the kitchen.

Daniel dropped a grass-coated tennis ball by the back door and the little dog followed him in. "Hey, bro. Looks like we both invited ourselves for dinner." The dog plopped on the tile, panting, paws stretched out.

"Can't beat Mom's meatloaf." Grayson set the last place setting.

Soon Dad joined them, and they all sat, said grace, and dug in. Hot and savory meatloaf melted in his mouth, and his shoulders relaxed. This was the best part of the whole day. A great ending to a mixed week.

He turned to Daniel. "What's with the dog?"

Daniel grimaced as he chewed. "My boss's dog is a pure-bred Yorkie. He breeds her with other papered dogs and sells her puppies. But I guess she got out, and he didn't know she was pregnant until it was too late. Since he can't sell them, he's been giving them away. But this one came back, and he's trying to find a home for him." He reached over and squeezed Grayson's shoulder. "You want a little dog, don't you? I told my boss I thought I could find him a home. It would score me some big points."

Grayson shrugged off Daniel's grip. "Really? What would I do with a dog? I'm gone all day."

"Yeah, but you live close enough to come home at lunch."

He did, but that wasn't the point. Daniel always got Grayson to get on board with his schemes and then took the credit while Grayson did the grunt work. The dog must have known they were talking about him. He trotted over to Grayson and nudged his leg. He looked part terrier, but his coat was more wiry and he had a cute little pig nose. A funny-looking little dog. Grayson reached down to pet him.

"What's his name?"

"Cam. Maybe short for Cameron? You could change it, I'm sure."

Cam's ears perked up. Or tried to. One still folded over a bit. He clearly knew his name.

Grayson shouldn't ask any more questions, but he couldn't help himself. "How old is he?"

"Four months. Fixed, has all his shots, and he's housebroken. Mostly."

Sure he was. Grayson sighed.

After dinner, he and Daniel helped Mom with the dishes while Dad turned on the news. The puppy trotted around their feet, mostly getting in the way. Grayson heard the newscaster say, "Have you seen this man? The Laguna Vista Police Department released these images today of a man suspected of vandalizing Samashima Farms on Sunday."

He joined Dad in the family room just as Cait's photos flashed across the screen. He waited for the report to end. Seemed like the police didn't have any new information. At least none that they were sharing. Had Cait known they were going to air the vandal's photo?

"I know something about that story." He sunk back into the deep leather couch, the cool leather seeping through his dress pants and shirt. The puppy jumped on his lap. Grayson petted him while glaring at a grinning Daniel who plopped next to him.

Mom joined them, and they listened while he told about knowing Cait from choir, giving her a ride, and then what he'd found out about the property.

"That poor girl!" Mom shook her head. "I can't imagine how scared she must have been coming across that man. She's lucky he didn't try to attack her instead of just smashing up her car."

He nodded. "I've thought that too. She's a pretty amazing woman, though. You should see the farmhouse she's rehabbing, mostly by herself." He told them of her projects and the progress she'd made. "I plan on heading over there tomorrow to see her gardens."

"Do you think she's in any danger still?" Mom asked. "If that man knows she took his picture, if he figures out who she is?"

"I've wondered about that myself. I'm just not sure what to do about it."

Dad looked over from his recliner. "Seems like you've done an awful lot for a girl you hardly know. Are you sure this isn't another one of your lost causes?" He glanced at the dog, though Grayson didn't know why since he hadn't agreed to take the dog.

He pushed down the irritation. Dad always thought Grayson couldn't finish any big project on his own and that he was a sucker for things that were beyond help. Yes, there had been a few projects when he was younger that he'd had to give up on. Or that Daniel had to help him with.

But he hadn't appreciated Dad stepping in and finishing his Pinewood Derby race car in Boy Scouts. Grayson would have finished it on his own. Instead of the blocky, paint-dripped cars all his friends had, his was smooth, rounded, and professionally painted. Clearly not his own work.

But he'd had his own moment of victory with the classic '69 Charger that sat in his garage. The one Dad had passed on as being beyond saving. Now it was fully restored and sat next to its modern counterpart.

At times like this, though, it seemed like Dad still thought of him as a twelve year old. He hoped that this development project would put that image to rest for good.

He swallowed to make sure his voice wasn't tight. "She's a friend from church that needs some help that I can provide. I don't think there's anything wrong with that. Plus, I've been interested in her for a while, so this is a good opportunity to get to know her better."

"Want some dessert?" Mom stood. "I have blueberry pie with vanilla ice cream."

"Sounds perfect." He sighed.

Mom patted his knee. "You have such a good heart, always wanting to help people." She patted the dog's head. "I think he likes you."

Dad grimaced. "And getting taken advantage of, as well."

"I don't think that's the case here, Dad." Grayson hoped that Cait could meet his parents someday, if things continued progressing between them. But this was not the impression he wanted them to have of her. And all the blueberry pie and ice cream in the world wouldn't make that bitter taste go away.

CHAPTER FIVE

CAIT'S PHONE DINGED, AND SHE tugged off her gardening glove before reaching for it in her back pocket. She perched on the edge of her wheeled garden cart studying the progress she had made. The side yard was looking good. The soil was ready to be worked, and then the fun part came: adding plants and flowers. She stretched out her legs to ease the ache.

It was a text from Grayson: U available? I'd love a tour of your garden & I can bring lunch. Charo Chicken ok?

She grinned and started to reply before she realized she would need a shower. Dirt rimmed her fingernails, even through the gloves. Though the day was cool, her shirt stuck to her back.

She texted back: Sounds great! Give me an hour?

See you then!

She gathered up her tools and stashed them under the wheeled cart's seat before tugging the whole thing back into the garage. On the back porch, she toed off her gardening clogs and headed to the kitchen sink, scrubbing her hands.

Some strawberries and cream would be a nice way to end

lunch. She had just enough time to cut some up and let them sit in a little sugar to make a nice syrup. For working for a strawberry farm, she never got tired of eating them. Having an unlimited supply—particularly of the ones that weren't pretty enough to sell—was one of the perks.

She rinsed and cut the strawberries, fingers flying over the familiar task. Her mind had been poring over the problems of the vandal, her house, and Grayson all morning. She was no closer to solving any of those issues than when she started, but at least her side yard looked good.

Grayson was really the only problem she had any control over. She enjoyed his company, and he had been nothing but kind to her. And he was interested in her and her projects. Was there a catch? She didn't tell too many people about her interests because when she did, they considered her old fashioned. She was. So what?

But back in high school, it hadn't been so pleasant. The few friends she had shared her hobbies with thought it was cool she could make so much stuff. Except Kayla. Even now, Cait could hear Kayla's sneering voice calling her Laura Ingalls for the rest of their school days. Lau-ra!

That memory floated to the surface anytime anyone asked about what she did with her free time or wanted to see the house. No one had been as mean as Kayla, but most people didn't understand it either.

Tossing the strawberry hulls into the pail that would go out to the compost pile, she put the bowl of sugared strawberries back into the fridge and hurried upstairs to jump in the shower. Grayson had seemed genuinely interested in her work on the house. He restored old cars, so he understood. But could there be more than that? Fear and anticipation chased each other through her chest as she quickly got ready.

She took a final glance at the Lone Star quilt that draped over the quilt rack at the foot of her bed. Taking a deep breath, she decided that for now, hope and anticipation should win out over fear. Just as the doorbell rang.

Grayson and Cait sat at the island in her kitchen pulling apart citrus-marinated grilled chicken and wrapping it up with fresh salsa in soft tortillas. It was one of his favorite meals, and he was glad Cait enjoyed it too. Sitting here with her was relaxed and comfortable.

"I've tried to make this before." Cait wiped her salsa-dripped hand with a napkin. "But I can't seem to get the marinade right. Still, like most kitchen experiments, even the mistakes are usually good to eat."

"Hey, I'll be your taste tester anytime. Would beat most of my meals, I'm sure." He piled another tortilla with chicken and salsa. "What did the Samashimas say when you talked to them?"

Cait took a sip of her iced tea. "They weren't too surprised. People have offered them a lot of money for their land over the years, and there have been some veiled threats. And they get the occasional ecoterrorist threat. Nothing this blatant, but Alani said they had received a couple of odd emails that they had dismissed as pranks. She was going to get them to Detective Taylor."

"Ecoterrorism? I hadn't thought of that. That's pretty much the opposite of someone who would want to develop the land."

She nodded. "Makoa is going to install more security cameras and hire a couple of guards to roam the property at night." She picked up the next-to-last bite of chicken. "It was interesting how at peace they were about it. Alani said over the years they came to believe the land was God's and they were simply the caretakers. He would protect the land or it would become whatever he chose it to be next." A moment of silence passed. "I want faith like that."

He watched her thoughts tumble behind her pale gray eyes. What would it be like to have a faith strong enough to trust calmly in God's next steps for his life? Something to ponder, anyway.

He popped the last bite of tortilla in his mouth and began cleaning up.

Cait hopped off her stool. "I have strawberries and cream for dessert, but I want to show you around first." Opening the back door, she moved through a small, covered porch and out into the backyard.

Raised beds dotted the backyard in even rows. Soft mulch crunched under his feet. Hand-lettered tags indicated what was growing, herbs and lettuces closest to the front, and spaces marked out for warmer-weather vegetables. The perimeter fence, an old decorative wire one, was dotted with perennials.

"There's not a lot out yet, but with California weather, there are some annuals I can grow year round. I'll be seeding my showy annual flowers around the fence soon. At the beginning of summer, it's in its full glory before the heat starts taking its toll."

They walked through the beds, and she led him through a small gate to the side yard. The freshly-turned dirt made it obvious she had been working here. She showed him the small, old garage that was only big enough to hold tools. Then they moved to the front yard, where she talked about what she had already done and what she hoped to do.

He was in awe of how her mind worked, seeing what needed to be done and creating a plan. It was similar to how he approached reconstructing an old car.

Avoiding the bad step, they headed up the front porch and back inside. His mind was whirling. He didn't want to leave, and she seemed to enjoy his company. He scanned the entryway with new eyes. The sun shone through the front door, lighting up dust motes but making the old wood glow.

A framed cross-stitch hung on the wall, cream background with red letters and a green and red vine twining around the border. UNLESS THE LORD BUILDS THE HOUSE, THE BUILDERS LABOR IN VAIN. PSALM 127:1. He tapped it lightly with his finger. "This is perfect for this house. Did you do it?"

Cait stepped closer to him, filling his nose with a hint of

exotic fruit. "My grandma made that. It was one of the verses we memorized together. She used to tell me that even though we use the work of our hands to make things, it's only by the grace of God that we can accomplish anything."

He touched her shoulder, pulling her closer. "She sounds like a wise woman. I would have liked to have met her."

He felt her nod. "She was." It came out softly.

They stood there for a moment, not moving. He didn't want to do anything to break the closeness that wrapped around them.

"Grayson?" She looked up at him. "Do you think they can find me? He could have gotten the license plate off my car."

The moment shattered like broken glass around their feet. He pulled her into his arms, setting his chin on her head. "I don't really know. It's been almost a week. I'm not sure what he'd gain by tracking you down."

She pushed back a bit, her hands resting on his chest, her gaze meeting his. "That's what the logical part of my brain says, but it's good to hear someone else say it too."

He held her gaze a moment longer then reached for her hand. "Show me that stained-glass window in the bathroom that I couldn't see the other night."

She smiled. "Okay."

The stairs creaked as they climbed. A bathroom with black and white tile stood at the top of the stairs.

She had shown it to him Wednesday night when he had gotten the full house tour. The look was updated classic. Hexagonal white tiles covered the floor while white subway tile with a black tile border acted as a wainscoting half way up the walls which were painted sunny yellow. An old dresser served as the vanity. A claw-foot tub and a shower in its own tiled enclosure kept the room functional while maintaining its vintage roots.

But sunlight streamed through a piece of framed stained glass hung in front of the window, spilling red and yellow light over the floor tiles. Magical.

"Genius." He leaned against the door frame. "It creates

privacy, but with it being in a south-facing window, you get this beautiful effect nearly all day long."

She grinned. "One of those lucky breaks you hope you get a lot of when you're remodeling."

They headed down the hallway. "I know what you mean. Once we were restoring a '57 Chevy. I pulled this gross plastic off the seats and found pristine, original upholstery."

To the right were two bedrooms that hadn't been touched. One had some significant water damage. The plaster had fallen off and exposed the lath behind it. The other had been painted a garish orange.

Cait grimaced. "I can't tell you how tempted I am to paint over that. I know there's no point, but it's hideous!"

He laughed. "So you keep the door shut. But the woodwork is still in beautiful condition. It escaped getting painted. Think of all the stripping that saves you."

"Oh I know."

On the opposite end of the hall were two more rooms. One in the same condition as the others. The final room was clearly Cait's. Pale blue walls with an antique bedroom set.

"I have something else to show you that doesn't show up at night. This is the best part." She led him through her room to the opposite side and opened a door. "A sun porch! It looks out over the backyard and sits over the back porch."

A narrow, window-lined room ran the length of her bedroom. It hadn't been finished yet, but it was clean and she had a reading chair and ottoman out there. "I bet you get a great breeze."

"Natural air-conditioning. It's my favorite spot in this house. I can't wait to get it finished so I can really enjoy it."

They moved back through her bedroom. At the foot of her bed was a quilt rack with a Lone Star quilt hung over it. He had noticed it the other night. "My mom has one of these in this same pattern. She bought it from an Amish store when she and her friends did a sight-seeing tour back East." He ran his hand over the stitching. "Pretty colors."

Cait took a step toward him and looked up. "Thanks. I made it. My grandma helped me, but I was so proud of myself when I had finished it."

"When did you make it?" When would she have had time with everything else she had going on?

"In high school." She touched the fabric. "Grandma and I spent hours on it. I treasure that time."

"I can't imagine how you found the time. I'm sure you were busy with school activities and your friends. I know I had less time to work on cars with all of that."

She sat on the bed and let out a sigh. "I was home alone a lot. My folks had divorced. My dad moved to Colorado, and my mom was busy working on her career and finding her next husband. So I spent a lot of time at Grandma's. She's really the one who raised me."

He frowned. "What about your friends? Football games? Clubs and activities?"

"I didn't do too much of that." She picked at the floral comforter on the bed. "I brought some friends home to show them this quilt. At the time, I didn't know it would be the last quilt Grandma and I would make together. I was so proud of how I had pieced all of this intricate geometry."

She touched the center of the quilt. "See how the star in the center seems to pulse because of the different diamond-shaped fabric pieces? I loved how the fabric seemed to come to life. A few of my friends thought it was cool that I could make bread, so I said I'd show them how and show them the quilt. But one girl kept goofing around and started calling me Laura Ingalls. So that was pretty much the end of my social life. I had a few friends, and that was fine."

He picked up her hand and kissed the back of it. "The quilt is amazing and so are you."

She stood and smiled. "Thanks for not thinking I'm weird."

He laughed. "Are you kidding? Hey, didn't you promise

me strawberries and cream?" He kept her hand in his as he tugged her out into the hallway and they headed downstairs to the kitchen.

After stuffing himself with the berries—he was full but they tasted so good, he couldn't stop eating them—he reluctantly got up to leave. He pulled Cait into a hug at the front door. "What do you think about lunch and a walk along the beach tomorrow after church?"

"I think it's a great idea. The water will be chilly, but the sun is out and it'll be gorgeous."

"Good. I'll pick you up for church. I have a surprise for you."

Chapter Six

A light tap on the front door caused Cait to jump out of the living room chair she'd been sitting in, sipping coffee. She hadn't heard Grayson's car. She looked out the window. A white construction truck was parked across the street. She frowned. Who would be having work done on a Sunday? Then she saw it. A black, classic 1969 Dodge Charger parked next to the curb. That must be the surprise he was talking about.

She hurried to the front door and pulled it open. "I didn't realize that was you."

Grayson stepped inside, dark-wash jeans and an untucked, light cotton shirt fitting his athletic form nicely. He pulled her into a loose hug and kissed her forehead. "Come see my baby." He slid his hand down to grasp hers.

She grabbed her purse and Bible and followed him out, locking the door behind them.

He showed her all around his car and told her what he'd done to it. "My dad thought it was a total loss, not worth fixing at all. And it probably wasn't, for all the time and money I've put into it. But I'm glad I did."

She nodded. He had done a beautiful job with the old car. "I think many restoration projects are more about love than value."

He opened the door for her, and she slid in, the smell of old, hot vinyl enveloping her. The old-style gauges on the dash reminded her of her grandma's old car. Grayson climbed in and cranked the engine. It rumbled to life, and they headed off to church.

She cracked her window to let a little air in. "So this is your Sunday car, huh? Nice surprise."

He grinned. "I'm glad you like it, but it's not the only surprise. That will have to wait until after church."

Now she was intrigued, but so far, her and Grayson's brains moved on the same wavelength, so she was sure she'd like the other surprise.

After church, Grayson pulled into a parking spot in front of his townhome. It was too hard for a passenger to get out of the Charger when it was in the garage. Not without dinging the door on the newer Charger that sat next to it. And he wanted to show Cait his place, especially since he knew so much about hers.

He helped her out, and they headed inside. It wasn't anything spectacular, but it was his. Whining and yapping greeted them the moment the door swung open.

Cait raised her eyebrows. "I didn't know you had a dog."

"Well, he's a recent acquisition you could say." He hurried over to the crate in the kitchen where the copper ball of fur wagged itself in circles. "This is Cam."

As soon as he released the latch, Cam bounded out the door, barely giving Grayson a sniff before zipping around the room at high speed, bouncing off the back of the couch, the dining room chairs, and finally trying to jump at Cait.

She took a step back and then picked him up, laughing. "He has a lot of energy."

Cam tried to lick her face, and she jerked back to avoid his tongue.

"And not a lot of manners yet." He gave her the brief story of how he had ended up with the dog. "If I can find him a better home, I'd gladly give him up. But he's nice once he settles down." He opened the slider to the small, enclosed backyard and Cam ran out, alternately sniffing and watering plants.

Grayson shrugged and shoved his hands in his pockets. "So… that is surprise number two."

She laughed. "He is kinda cute, in a funny looking way. And he's really friendly. I bet he will be good company for you."

He gave her a quick tour, though there wasn't much to see. A kitchen, dining, and living area with a half bath made up the downstairs, and the upstairs had dual master suites. He hadn't done a ton of decorating, but it was clean, understated, and comfortable.

"I can picture you here," Cait said as they came back downstairs. "Ever had a roommate in that other suite?"

"No, but I bought it with that possibility in mind. My brother, Daniel, stayed here once for about six months. I think it was the longest six months of both our lives."

"Ah, so now I'm glad I'm an only child."

He gave her a half grin. "I thought I'd bring Cam to the beach with us." He gathered up a leash that sat on top of the crate. "Maybe wear him out. If that's possible."

"Sounds like fun."

He whistled, and Cam came running back in, jumping up and down when he saw the leash. Grayson could hardly get the leash clipped to Cam's collar, he was wiggling so much.

In one hand, Grayson grabbed a cooler he had packed with drinks and snacks before church and with the other, wrangled Cam's leash. He ushered everyone out the door and into the car. Cam immediately claimed Cait's lap, and she rolled the window down a bit for him to stick his nose out.

Grayson headed the car toward the beach. "I know a great sandwich place where we can grab lunch."

"Sounds good."

He let out a breath and glanced at Cait. While the wind tossed strands of her hair, she scratched Cam's ears as he panted contentedly. She clearly liked the first surprise of the day. He wasn't entirely sure how she felt about the second, but she was a good sport regardless. Now he just had to find a way to spend more time with her.

In the car heading home from the beach, Cait struggled to keep her eyes open. The sun warmed the car and created the perfect temperature for a nap. Her stomach was still full from the huge roast beef sandwich she had eaten. Then they had walked Cam all along the beach walk. It didn't seem possible, but the little guy had run out of energy. He was asleep on her lap. She was almost there with him, worn out from the walking and the sun.

But talking to Grayson would help keep her awake, and she wanted to use this time to get to know him better. "Tell me more about that big project you're working on."

He explained about his clients' needs and how he had a vision for creating a bigger project if he could get all the players together. "I've got a meeting set for this week, and I just need DiMarco construction to confirm that they'll be there. They are the big fish in this pond, and I can't pull off a project of this scale without them."

"I guess it's not much of a coincidence then that they tried to buy my farmhouse as part of their subdivision." She covered a yawn with her hand. "How did you decide to become a real estate attorney, since your passion is fixing old cars?"

He chuckled. "Not a lot of money in restoring old cars,

except for a few people. And you can bang your knuckles up pretty good." He reached over for her hand and took it in his. "I like details and putting projects together, seeing possibilities that others can't see. I was majoring in business when I did an internship with a friend of my dad's who was a real estate attorney. I seemed to have a knack for the project development side of it, and he offered me a job after school.

"I think the car thing started out as being more about finding a way to be with my dad and make him proud. Big brother Daniel was always the star of the show. So any time I could get out from under his shadow, I did."

She squeezed his hand and smiled. "More and more I'm seeing the advantages of being an only child."

"Daniel and I are closer now, but back in high school when I was a freshman and he was a senior, he was great at sports and I was better at academics. I had this huge display I had created for the science fair all about the combustion engine. It was a large part of my grade, and I was proud of it. I was taking it to the car so I could set it up at school. Daniel and a couple of his friends were goofing around, playing football in the front yard."

She knew where this was going. Dread and sympathy filled her chest.

"Yep. A football right through my display. Completely ruined. Not enough time to fix it, and I ended up with a C. Daniel didn't get in trouble. Dad actually blamed me, said I should have known better than to carry it out when Daniel and his friends were out there."

So she wasn't the only one whose parents couldn't see what their kids were going through. "That was really rotten."

He nodded. "I guess that's why I'm obsessed with every detail now. Making sure nothing can go wrong." He patted the Charger's dash. "This baby proved that I did have good judgment and could see how to make something out of nothing. But it's only a hobby. This land development project I'm putting together... that's the real deal."

"I don't doubt it. Sounds like we've both received a lot of grief for seeing something where most people see nothing."

His thumb traced over her hand. "And hopefully we have more positive things in common too. But speaking of making something out of nothing, I was thinking I could help you repair that dining room floor. I've seen some pretty gross things in cars, so I think I could handle your root cellar. You could do the work up top."

Warmth flooded her chest. It was rare for anyone to offer help. Usually she had to beg and bribe. Most people didn't want to get sucked into what they thought of as her money pit. So she only asked for help as a last resort. "Are you sure? Because that would be great."

"Of course. I love seeing something change with a little bit of work. Hard to see tangible results like that in my job. Or they are a long time coming."

She nodded. He understood her heart in a way no one since Grandma had. She blinked back tears. "Name your dessert, and I'll make it for you."

"Ooh, bribe me with food, and I'll do anything."

Swallowing, she gave him a soft smile. Her instincts were right. All those weeks ago when they had spent several Christmas-time services talking, all she could think was how great he seemed and how much she wanted him to ask her out. And then nothing had happened. Until now.

They pulled up in front of her house. Cam must have sensed the car stopping, since he stood on her lap and shook himself, yawning. She wrapped his leash around her hand and stepped out.

"Wait." Grayson's hand held her back. "What happened to your front porch?"

Cam hopped out of the car and strained at the end of his leash, sniffing everything in reach.

"What?" She peered around Grayson. Her porch steps no longer existed. They had been in bad shape, but they shouldn't have just collapsed. And her planting beds were all torn up. The wooden screen door flopped on one hinge. What had happened? It didn't make any sense.

Her legs turned to water. *He* had found her. The vandal. He had figured out where she lived and come after her. She collapsed on the car seat. What else had he done?

"Stay here. I'm going to check things out. Hand me your keys. Then we should call the cops. Do you have that detective's card with you?"

She handed over her keys, nodding then shook her head. "No. I'm not sure. I think it's on my desk inside. Or at work. I can't remember."

"I'll be right back." He squeezed her shoulder. "Get your phone out."

Fumbling through her purse was difficult with Cam pulling on the leash and jerking her hand around. She snagged her phone and set it in her lap. Where had she had that card last? At work. She scrolled through her recent call list, looking for one that might be his. Yep, she looked at the date and time. This was it.

Grayson came out through the front door, using his shirt to hold the knob, gingerly pushing the broken screen door aside. "He's not here, and he didn't get inside the house. Do you have the detective's number?"

"Yes, in my call log."

He took the phone from her, and she heard him explain to the detective what he'd found. Vandalism, he said. Some paint on the side of her house.

What? She looked up at Grayson, but he merely slipped his arm around her shoulder and pulled her close, still listening to the detective. She could hear bits and pieces of the detective's words, and it sounded like he said something about Mario and the farm. She bounced her leg, wishing Grayson would hurry up and end the call.

Finally, he handed the phone back to her. "He'll be here

soon, and he's sending some officers over. Let me show you what I found." He took Cam's leash from her, and slid his arm around her waist.

She got a better look at the damage to her lovely camellias. All the verbena had been dug up. It might replant okay. But the poppies were gone. Why do this in broad daylight? Wouldn't he be concerned a neighbor would think this destruction was odd?

Her steps had been destroyed with a saw; she could see the clean cut. Her mind flashed to someone who might not look out of place cutting up things in her yard. A construction worker. A shudder ran through her. "Grayson! This morning there was a white construction truck parked across the street. He had been watching me, waiting for me to leave."

He pulled her closer. "That would explain a few things."

They rounded the house to the side yard. GET OUT! in blood-red dripping paint covered nearly all of the two-story siding.

She clamped a hand over her mouth, afraid she was going to be sick.

As Detective Taylor toured the damage, Grayson kept clenching and unclenching his fists. His mind was already tallying up the damage and developing a plan for fixing things.

"Maybe we could go inside to talk." Detective Taylor motioned to the house.

Cait nodded, leading the way through the garden and up the back steps. At least her garden had been spared.

At the end of the leash Grayson still held, Cam sniffed then bounded up the steps inside.

"Water? Iced tea?" She stood in front of the refrigerator, looking at him and the detective in turn.

"No, thanks." Taylor settled on the barstool at the kitchen counter and opened his notebook.

She motioned to Cam. "You can let him explore. I don't think there's anything he can hurt."

Grayson unclasped the leash and the little dog took off, following his nose around the baseboards and into the dining room.

Taylor waited for Cait to sit. "The same thing happened to your farm manager, Mario, while he and his family were at church. Then, it looks like whoever did this headed over to the farm after the store had closed. He must have been watching the guards or was lucky that he was able to do his damage there during a time when they couldn't see him. We did get him on the security cameras, but he's wearing a baseball cap and kept his face turned where we couldn't see him. But based on his build, he looks an awful lot like the guy you got a picture of breaking open the irrigation valves."

"Did he do that again? What kind of damage was there to the farm?" Cait gripped her hands together.

Grayson slid his hand over hers and gently squeezed.

Taylor shook his head. "Not as much as last time. Just the same spray-painted message. Any idea why his message was 'get out'?"

She slowly shook her head. "No. Get out of what? It doesn't make any sense to me at all. Does it line up with any of the email threats the Samashimas had received?"

"Possibly. Like this message, they were vaguely threatening."

"Kinda sounds like ecoterrorism." Grayson shifted on his barstool. "On a very mild scale. We get that sometimes when people don't want areas developed, thinking some sort of wildlife might be threatened by a project. Or they just don't want any development at all. Do you think they want to drive the farm out of business?"

"It's hard to say. You'd think whoever is doing this would be more explicit in their demands." Taylor put his notebook away and slid off the stool. "We got a shoe print in your side yard garden. I'll see if we can step up patrols in this area and by Mario's house and the farm."

Cait let out a breath. "I can see why I might be hit. The guy that trashed my car could have gotten my license plate number and figured out where I live. I was afraid that would happen. But why Mario? How would anyone know that he had anything to do with the farm?"

"That's a good question." The detective headed for the back door. "If you think of anything, call me. I'll let you know as soon as I know anything."

Grayson shook hands with him. "Hey, you know Bernie Sanchez, don't you?"

"Yeah, we're in a Bible study together."

"I know him from choir at church."

Taylor's eyes lit up. "That's why you both seem so familiar. I've seen you sing at church."

"Come back by the green room and say hi sometime. A bunch of us often grab lunch after the last service."

"I'll have to do that." Taylor pushed opened the door and left.

Grayson turned to see Cait with her head in her hands. He rubbed her back. "Let me get us some of that iced tea. Don't worry; I've got a plan."

She nodded but didn't lift her head.

He poured them glasses of iced tea thinking of what he could do to make her feel better. Not much, probably. But there had to be something. He slid the glass in front of her.

She raised her head and smiled. "Thanks." Big sigh. "I had hoped I had escaped this guy, that the first incident was just a random act. But now he's found me and done even more damage. I don't know what to do next."

"All you have to do tonight is figure out what will make you feel safe enough to sleep." He rubbed her arm. "I'll leave Cam with you." He grinned. "At least you'll know if anyone is coming."

She gave him a soft smile. "That's sweet. I think I would feel better with the little guy around. I wonder where he is."

"Sniffing out every creature that's ever been in this house.

Probably wearing out his nose."

Her smile widened, exactly the effect he was hoping for.

He tugged on her hand. "Why don't we take our drinks outside and you can show me the best place to watch the sunset?"

"Good idea."

He grabbed their glasses, and she led him to the bench at the back of her garden. "This is one of my favorite spots. Secluded from the neighbors, but if you lean forward a bit, you can see the sky change colors."

They settled in, and he draped his arm across her shoulder. The silence between them settled comfortably as she relaxed against his shoulder.

"It's going to be okay, you know."

Her head moved against him. "I know. It's just so much right now. I had plenty to do before having to fix stuff that was already fixed. On top of that, if the farm loses income, I lose income. I was hoping to get a few more restaurants on board with the farm-to-table so I could fix the house's electrical. Until that's done, I can't move forward on any other big projects."

His heart pounded in his chest. Could she hear it? "Cait."

When he didn't say anything else, she turned to look at him.

He took her face in his hands. "You're not in this alone. I'll help you. I'm not going to leave you until you tell me to." His thumb moved over her soft cheek.

Her lips parted, and her eyes softened.

Lowering his head, he touched his lips to hers. They were as soft and sweet as he had imagined. Every bit of tenderness in his heart longed to be expressed. He pulled her a little closer before releasing her.

Her eyes slowly opened. A soft smile crossed her face.

Now, that kiss was a surprise he enjoyed as much as she did.

Chapter Seven

Cait tossed the Jitter Bug cup in her office trash and tried to concentrate on her computer screen. She wasn't having any luck. Just like she didn't have any luck last night falling asleep. With the memories of Grayson's kiss and the vandalism of her house chasing each other through her head, it was the early hours in the morning before her exhausted brain gave up and went to sleep.

The good news was she had gotten her car back today. Alani had helped her pick it up and return the rental. Being out and about had helped wake her up a bit.

Maybe she needed another coffee. She wandered out to the break room and grabbed a cup. Not as good as Jitter Bug's, but decent.

Of course, her thoughts weren't the only things keeping her up. The once-comforting creaks of her house now made her wonder if the vandal was back. Plus, her new little roommate wasn't too happy with being confined to his crate. Grayson had brought it over with Cam's food, dishes, and favorite toy. He howled and whined until she relented and set him free. He hopped up the stairs behind her. She had put down an old blanket for him with one of his toys on the floor next to her bed, but as soon as she was in bed, he leaped up to join her, claiming the extra pillow. She was too tired to make him get down. Plus, knowing he would serve as an early warning system allowed her to finally close her eyes.

How was little Cam doing without her today? She had put him back in his crate with his toy. Maybe if she weren't around, he'd settle down. She'd check on him at lunch.

Coffee refilled, she made her way back to her office, steps slow, as if she might have some great revelation on the way.

Arm outstretched, Rachel stopped her. "This is for you. A reporter from the *South County News* wants a comment on the vandalism."

Cait took the paper and blew out a breath. Great, that was all she needed. More publicity. Website views had been up since the first incidence of vandalism. Traffic was up a bit at the farm store. But customers and vendors had both been calling, skittish about what the farm's troubles could mean for them.

"Thanks, Rachel. I'll handle it." Once in her office, Cait plopped in her chair. She'd much rather be thinking about Grayson's kiss—and when it might happen again—instead of dealing with this mess that she couldn't wrap her mind around.

One piece that didn't make sense was Mario. Why him? She clicked on the farm's website and went to the About Us page. There was a small bio on each of their full-time employees that emphasized the family nature of the farm. Mario was there with a photo, but no last name or indication of where he lived.

She glanced at the message slip with the reporter's name on it. With all the inquiries, she should at least check the farm's website to make sure all was up to date. Clicking on the Media tab, she scrolled through their media kit and the latest, positive articles about the farm.

She stopped scrolling.

There. The same reporter, Monica West, who wanted a call back, had done an article on the farm a year ago. Cait thought her name had sounded familiar. But it was a Features section piece, interviewing the Samashimas and talking about the farm's history and its family tradition.

Her eyes skimmed the article. If she remembered correctly ... Yep, there it was. A couple of paragraphs on her and Mario and their hobbies outside of work. It talked about Cait's restoration of her farmhouse and Mario's love of cooking.

And then this comment by Alani: "We couldn't run this place a day without them."

Cait's stomach grew as heavy as her favorite cast-iron skillet. Was this why they had been targeted? Another attempt to take the farm down? Did someone take Alani's words literally, assuming the farm would stop operation if Cait and Mario left?

She reached for her cell phone then stopped. Was it too ridiculous of an idea to run by Detective Taylor? On the face of it, did it sound egotistical, like she was so important that if she ran scared the farm would collapse? That was ridiculous.

Wasn't it?

She reached for her phone again, finger hovering over Grayson's number: the other subject she had tossed around in her head last night. Not only his kiss, but the fact that he wanted to help. He didn't have to, but he made it clear he was sticking around. Hope floated in her chest like a soap bubble, and it felt as fragile.

Could she trust him with her latest idea on the vandalism? Would he think she was ridiculous?

Only one way to find out. She swallowed and touched his number before she lost her nerve.

For a Monday, it was pretty great. Grayson had already fielded a call from Tony DiMarco. He was interested and wanted to talk about the project over lunch.

And of course, the kiss he'd shared with Cait hadn't been far from his thoughts. She was special, and he wanted her to be a part of his life. He just wished he could guarantee he could keep her safe, a thought he knew was ridiculous the moment it entered his brain. Still, he wanted the vandal caught so he and Cait could put her house back in order and move forward with their lives without worrying about this guy.

His phone buzzed and Cait's number appeared. This was definitely a great Monday.

"I hope I'm not disturbing you. I came up with an idea about the vandal. I have to let Cam out at lunch, so I wondered if you had time to grab something to eat and I could run my idea by you." Her voice held a thread of nervousness. What had happened now?

The brightness of his day collapsed. "Oh man, I wish I could. I have a lunch meeting with Tony DiMarco about that big project. He seems genuinely interested so I need to follow through. Can you tell me your idea now? I have some time."

She told him her theory, and he brought up the farm's website while she was talking. "It's an interesting idea. I think it's as solid as anything else they have to go on. You should call Detective Taylor and let him know."

"Okay, thanks for the vote of confidence. I was too close to this thing to be sure if it wasn't just my desire to make some sense out of this."

"It's smart thinking. Maybe the cops can do something with it." He paused. "I'm sorry about lunch. It would have been great. I'll bring by ice cream tonight to make it up to you."

Cait brushed away his concerns, and they hung up. But something in her voice made him wonder if he'd let her down.

Cam's barking reached Cait's ears before she could get the back door open. He was wiggling like his tail was on fire as she let him out of his crate. He shot out and alternated between zipping around the room and coming back to sniff her. On one of his trips back to her, she snagged him and clipped on his leash. As soon as she opened the back door, he dashed out, yanking her along.

They wandered among her garden beds while Cam sniffed and peed. He never stopped yanking on the leash. If he was going to stay with her, he would need some training. She'd have to look into it.

It was nice having this break in the middle of the day. She had an excuse to walk around her yard and let her mind wander. She had been disappointed Grayson wasn't available for lunch. For some reason, she had assumed he would be. She'd garnered so much of his attention lately, she'd taken it for granted. But he had his big project he was working on, and she wanted him to succeed at that, even if it meant she got less of his attention.

Still, it stung a bit and left a hole in her day. Both feelings were unexpected and unnerved her. She was too dependent on him too fast. Yes, he had followed through on his promise and wanted to help her. But whether he continued to remained to be seen. She needed to guard her heart.

But he was going to bring her ice cream tonight, so it certainly didn't seem like he was dodging her.

It had been a full morning anyway. After talking to Grayson, she had enough nerve to call Detective Taylor. He listened to her and didn't call her crazy, so that was a good thing. She sent him the website link. At the last minute, she thought to tell him about Monica West's latest request for an interview and ask his advice.

"Keep the information you tell her to general facts," he

had said. "Refer her to me for more specifics."

Which is exactly what she did. Ms. West wasn't thrilled about not getting any juicy details, but there weren't any to give.

She led Cam out to the side yard. The boot print was still visible. Cam sniffed that bed too. Maybe he'd get a scent and help catch the vandal. She gave a small laugh. Cam looked up at her, which made her laugh louder. His ears twitched. Poor guy, he probably thought she was laughing at him.

Her laugh ended in a sigh as she took in the words painted on her house. That would take some scrubbing. Guess that was on her agenda for tonight. Along with trying to replant the verbena in the front.

"Come on, Cam. Let's take a lap around the house, and then I need to grab some lunch and get back to work." She tugged on his leash, and he headed to the front. She hated to look at the disaster it had become. Maybe bringing Cam this way wasn't a good idea. But he was already sniffing the front porch.

She surveyed the damage again. The insurance company's adjuster still hadn't called her back. But with her high deductible, she'd be paying for a lot of this out of her own pocket, not to mention the sweat equity.

The wooden screen door still swung lazily. She should take it down and see if it could be repaired. She loved that old door.

Something was taped to the small brick wall where the stairs used to start. She grabbed the paper and flipped it open.

YOUR DOG HAS BEEN BARKING ALL DAY. DO SOMETHING ABOUT IT OR I'M GOING TO CALL ANIMAL CONTROL.

Crumpling the paper in one hand, she pulled on Cam's leash with the other.

What a Monday.

Grayson leaned back in his chair at the restaurant where they had just finished eating lunch. Tony DiMarco seemed pleased with the presentation. And if he got on board, everyone else would too.

DiMarco crossed his arms, the fabric of his custom-made Italian shirt bunching at the elbows. "I like it. That was pretty ingenious thinking to link those two parcels. If all goes well, we all stand to make a killing."

Grayson nodded, trying to keep cool but inwardly excited that someone else had finally caught his vision. And the money wouldn't be bad either.

Since DiMarco was pleased, Grayson moved the map on his screen over and pointed. "Now if we could ever get our hands on this parcel …" He watched DiMarco's face, but the man was inscrutable.

"Yeah, people have been trying for years, but they'll never sell that farm. I can't imagine what kind of persuasion it would take."

"Any idea who might be trying to persuade them currently?"

"Who wouldn't, if they thought it would work? Anyone would kill to get their hands on that property." He held Grayson's gaze for a moment, then, "Back to the original project, I just have a few … suggestions."

"Okay." Grayson took notes as DiMarco's "suggestions" got more involved. Some of these were things he really didn't want to do, but it wouldn't do to balk at it now. He'd thought through these contingencies and made different decisions. He pushed back on a few, explaining his reasoning, but clearly Tony DiMarco was a man used to having things his way or not at all.

Finished jotting down DiMarco's ideas, Grayson closed his laptop. He had one more idea flitting around his brain.

"That single-family housing development you did over off Cedar Ridge?" At DiMarco's nod, he continued. "How did you manage to let that farmhouse get excluded?"

"What do you know about that?" DiMarco cocked his head.

Grayson shrugged. "I met the owner."

DiMarco pursed his lips. "She had gotten to it before we did. And then she was unwilling to sell, no matter how much I offered her. Quite a piece of work." He waited a beat. "She works for the Samashimas, doesn't she? Seems like they're cut out of the same cloth." He stood. "I'll look for your revised proposal by the end of this week."

Grayson shook DiMarco's hand and then watched him walk away. As he packed up his computer and notepad, he wondered if he had done the right thing mentioning the farm and Cait's house. DiMarco was no dummy. He knew Grayson was fishing. And he knew more than he was telling. The question was how much more?

He rubbed his face. He was going to have to cancel getting ice cream with Cait tonight. It would be a minor miracle if he could make all DiMarco's changes by the end of the week. But it would leave Saturday for him to fix Cait's porch steps. She would understand.

And he hoped DiMarco was only speaking figuratively when he said anyone would kill to get their hands on the Samashima farm.

Chapter Eight

Cait came back from the staff meeting to find Cam curled up in her office chair. It was his favorite spot. Or, if she happened to need her chair, he crawled under her desk. Luckily, he had been good mannered at work, and it hadn't been a problem with anyone to have him here.

She rattled his leash, and his head popped up. She snapped it on him and led him outside. He could use a potty break, and she could use some fresh air. They walked down one of the farm access roads, Cait breathing in deep of the damp, earthy air.

Even though Cam had been a good guest, she still couldn't figure out who had left the note. Her lot was much larger than any of the others in the neighborhood, giving her a good buffer between her house and her neighbors. She couldn't figure out how anyone could hear him barking unless they were standing in her yard. And if so, why leave a note basically advertising they'd been trespassing?

It was just one more piece in her life that increasingly made no sense.

At least the insurance adjustor had made it out, and she'd scrubbed most of the paint off, though a faint trace would remain until she could repaint her house. Something else to add to her to-do list.

She'd talked to Grayson each night this week. He'd been too busy with his project, but he was excited that now it looked like it would become a reality. She was happy for him; she knew that feeling of facing an improbable situation, finding a solution, and then seeing it come to fruition. It was immensely satisfying.

Plus, he had committed to coming over Saturday to work on her porch steps. She was already planning a lunch of grilled chicken, fruit salad, potato salad, and chocolate cake with fudge icing. If he was going to put in a hard day's work, the least she could do was feed him well. It surprised her how much she missed him. He wouldn't be at choir practice tonight because of the project, and it would be strange not to see his face in the tenor section.

They headed back toward the farm office. Cait let Cam run the full length of the leash, and she let her thoughts wander while the sun warmed her shoulders and released the tension.

A quick bark and the leash yanked out of her fingers. Her thoughts jerked back to the present to see Cam take off after a rabbit, clearly the terrier in him in control.

"Cam!" She took off after him, but she had zero chance of his listening to her or catching him. The best she could hope for was to keep her eye on him until he lost his prey or wore himself out.

Except that he was headed for the barn. The rabbit ducked under a stack of wood and Cam sniffed it mightily. She had almost caught up to him and lunged for the leash when the clucking chickens caught his attention. He darted off, barking all around the chicken enclosure, darting back and forth. With his attention on the chickens, she closed the gap and stepped on his leash, holding it down while he tried to take off.

He looked back at her, confused, and she snatched up the leash. "Don't chase the chickens."

As if he understood, he cocked his head. He leaped up at her.

"Cam!" Muddy paw prints covered her pants and blouse. "Ugh!"

She glanced at her watch. A conference call in a few minutes meant she'd be stuck with muddy clothes; there wouldn't be time to go home and change. She blew out a sigh. Grayson meant well in giving her Cam, but it was a complicated gift.

Grayson tossed his keys and a bag of fast food on the counter of his kitchen. His eyes burned and his shoulders hurt from being hunched over a computer most of the day keeping up with his regular work load and the DiMarco project. But the end was in sight.

He slid into a chair and started eating. He missed Cait. Was he paying too high of a price for this project? It was the first time he'd ever considered that kind of question. A project like this didn't come along often, so he had to take advantage of it while he could. In the future, though, he couldn't imagine making this kind of sacrifice on a regular basis. It was why he chose the law firm and specialty that he did.

What time was it anyway? He glanced at his phone. Cait should be home from choir practice now. He touched her number, thinking he needed to get a photo of her for his phone.

Her voice was soft in his ear, but she sounded glad to hear from him. She told him about her latest adventures with Cam at the farm. He laughed at the rabbit-chasing story, but sensed some of her frustration with Cam's energy and mess-making capabilities.

A stab of regret shot through him. She didn't need the hassle of an active puppy on top of everything else. But he pushed it down. He couldn't take Cam now either. Not with his work schedule. The silence grew a bit taut.

"Also I got some other great news." Sarcasm dripped through the phone. "I came home to a notice of a code violation for my porch stairs. I have to pay a one-hundred-fifty-dollar fine, remediate the problem within ten days, and pay another seventy-five-dollar re-inspection fee when they come out to make sure I've done the work up to code. And since the steps were completely destroyed, I have to rebuild them to code instead of just repairing them."

"No! What on earth? Why would they even come out to your house in the first place?"

"Someone made a complaint. Probably the same person who complained about Cam's barking. Frankly, it's probably the vandal. He's determined to make my life miserable. What am I supposed to do? Quit working at the farm? How would that help?" Discouragement had pushed over the outrage in her voice. He hated that. None of this was fair. She didn't deserve to have any of these things happen to her.

"Oh, Cait. I'm so sorry. I wish I could hug you and make everything better. But I will be there Saturday to fix the steps. We'll figure out what we need to do to bring them up to code. Between the two of us, we can handle it." He smiled. They did make a good team.

A big sigh. "I know. And I appreciate your help more than you know. I'll even pay you with a great lunch."

He glanced at the greasy sack his dinner had come in. "I know it'll be way better than what I have been eating." His eyes burned, and he knew they both needed to call it a night. It was unsatisfying to leave her without any real comfort, but he didn't know what else he could do.

She seemed to sense it too. Without a sense of satisfaction, they awkwardly ended the call.

He tossed his phone on the table and sighed. He couldn't wait for this project with DiMarco to get the green light. Then he'd have more time to focus on Cait and why someone wanted to harass her.

Chapter Nine

Cait stared out the front window at the rain pouring down. She wanted to cry. No way they could fix the porch steps today, and she only had until next Thursday. The only question was, should she call Grayson and cancel? If he couldn't fix her porch steps, maybe he could use the time on his presentation.

On the other hand, she hadn't seen him all week. Was she being selfish?

It was a moot point because his car pulled into her driveway.

She headed to the kitchen so she could let him in the back door. Cam was already going nuts, wiggling so hard he couldn't sit down. As soon as she opened the door for Grayson, Cam took off like a shot. That dog! He splashed down the back steps, not even giving Grayson more than a passing sniff. Then around the garden beds, splashing mud all over himself. She had purposely let him out on a leash this morning so he would have to stay under the porch overhang and wouldn't get muddy.

Grayson hung up his wet coat on a hook in her enclosed back porch and toed off his shoes before pulling her into a hug and kissing her forehead. "I missed you. Want me to go get the dog?"

Being in his embrace gave her a sense of security and rightness. She didn't want to leave. She didn't want to talk about the dog. She didn't want to talk about the house. She'd like it to all go away. Reluctantly, she pulled back, glancing around him through the window where she saw Cam out in the mud and rain.

"No, he's as wet and muddy as he's going to get. Might as well let him enjoy it."

He squeezed her arm. "So, since we have a rain delay, do you have any thoughts? We could work on that dining room floor."

She shuddered. "Ick. Not in this rain. Who knows what creatures will come climbing out down there? Plus, I don't know if I have enough wood to patch it, and if we ran out, we'd have to stop and let it acclimate anyway."

He laughed. "We could always watch a movie."

She had been turning this dilemma over in her brain since she'd heard the rain when she woke up. "It's supposed to last all day and into tomorrow. I don't think there's anything we can do." Her stomach clenched. "I'm just afraid we won't get it done in time."

"I'll be here every night after work. I finished making all DiMarco's changes around midnight. The whole group has a meeting set for Tuesday. Hopefully, we can get the ball rolling from there."

She knew she struggled with having her plans changed. But there wasn't anything they could do about it. She should enjoy this time she had with him and trust that somehow God would allow them to make the repairs in time.

A slow smile spread across her face. "Okay. I'll make some coffee to go with the blueberry muffins I had made for us. Of course, I also made a huge lunch, thinking we would be burning a lot of calories. So, we may just eat our way through this day."

"That's my girl." He pulled her into a long hug that moved

into light kisses on her neck, cheek, and finally her lips. They became deeper, more tender, as all the pent-up emotion of not being able to spend time together poured out.

It took a moment for the noise to penetrate her brain. Scratching at the back door. Cam.

Wet, muddy dog always added to the romantic atmosphere. With a sigh, she pulled away and went to tackle the mess that was Cam.

It had turned out to be one of the nicest days Cait had had in a long time. And that wasn't something she had expected when she woke up this morning. Grayson had helped her bathe and dry Cam, as well as mop up the mud the dog had tracked in. Then he had gotten her hooked on a Netflix series, and they had binge watched their way through several episodes before lunch.

She was putting lunch away while he was letting Cam out—on his leash—during a break in the rain. A buzzing sounded, and she turned to see Grayson's phone light up on the kitchen island. A text.

"Grayson! You got a text."

He hadn't heard her. She peeked around the corner to the back porch. No Grayson and no Cam. Hmm. A look out the dining room window showed Grayson setting the dog on the concrete, keeping the leash tight. Aw, he was making sure he stayed out of the mud. And since the dining room windows were painted shut, she would have to put her gardening clogs on and go outside to inform him of the text.

It probably wasn't important. People get texts all the time. But what if it was about that big project he had been working on? People expected to be able to reach you immediately.

The phone buzzed again; this time it was an incoming phone call. Maybe it was an emergency. Feeling like she was snooping, she glanced at the screen. Tony DiMarco. That was the developer. This must be important. The call went to voice mail, and the text showed on the screen again.

Call me ASAP. Got info on the farm and farmhouse to our benefit.

Her stomach sunk, and she slid on to a barstool. She reread the text, certain she must be reading it wrong. Was Grayson involved in the vandalism? He couldn't be the vandal; he didn't fit the body type. But did this big project he was working on involve taking the farm away from the Samashimas? Was that the point of the vandalism, to get them all to give up? Had he just gotten close to her to feed information to whomever was behind the vandalism? She was going to be sick. Her mind rolled through all their times together, their kisses. Had they meant nothing?

The back door squeaked open, and she heard Grayson come in with Cam, hang up the leash, take off his shoes. Cam ran in and panted by her legs, but she couldn't look at him.

Grayson came up behind her and squeezed her shoulders, planting a kiss on her cheek. She stiffened.

He pulled back. "What's wrong?"

She shoved his phone at him. "Tell me there's an explanation for this. One that doesn't involve you feeding this guy information about me so he can ruin my life."

"What are you talking about?" He read the text. "I don't know what he means. When we were at lunch, I probed him for some information. He's the one that has the most to gain if the farm goes under. He's got developments all around, owns some vacant land, and has the most capital to buy the farm quickly. He admitted to wanting the farm, but said that everyone else did too."

He slid onto the barstool next to her, but she wouldn't look at him. What he said made sense, but it also sounded like a good cover story. "What about the farmhouse? What does he mean by that? Because it sounds an awful lot like my house."

"I suppose it is, though I don't know what he means by any of this being favorable to our project. I asked him how he let this house get away. I wanted to see what he would say, if it would be anything that would indicate he had any thoughts of revenge against you or wanted to force you out. He doesn't like you, but I didn't get any sense that he was trying to run you out of your house."

She dropped her head in her hands. She wanted to believe him, but she'd heard too many excuses and logical explanations from her parents for their actions. Bottom line was she still sat alone in the dark with only the TV for company far too many nights. Excuses came cheap.

This week it had been pretty obvious Grayson's priority was his project. What exactly was he willing to sacrifice to make it happen? Was she simply one more problem to solve?

"Cait, you have to believe me. I don't know what else I can tell you."

The pleading in his voice threatened to crack her composure. What if he was telling her the truth? Her emotions piled up in her chest, making it difficult to breathe. She needed to be alone to sort this out.

"I'd like you to leave." She didn't look at him; if she did, the look she imagined in his eyes would undo her resolve.

"Cait, please. Let's talk about this. I don't want to leave things this way between us."

She swallowed. "I can't. Not right now. Maybe later."

He didn't move. After what felt like an eternity, he slid off the stool, picked up his phone, and made his way out the back door. Until she heard his car start up and drive away, she didn't lift her head. Tears coursed down her cheeks, and sobs burst from her chest. She wanted more than anything to be wrong about Grayson, but in her experience, people were selfish and didn't care if you ended up as collateral damage. No, it didn't pay to let people close to you.

Grayson left Cait's house baffled by how such a good day could turn into such a mess. He drove home and flopped on to his couch, completely unsure what to do next. He reread DiMarco's text. What in the world could he mean? He listened to the voice message which said the same thing. What was going on?

So, did he call DiMarco and find out what he meant? He wanted to think this through first. He didn't want to do any more damage than he already had.

And regardless of that, how could he prove to Cait that he had nothing to do with the vandalism? He could see her point, in a way. He had started spending time with her after the first act of vandalism. But that was because she needed a ride. If he'd had his way, he would have been dating her right after Christmas.

And he was doing a big development deal that needed DiMarco as the key player. And DiMarco was the one that stood to gain the most if the farm was sold. And if her house was sold. But Grayson was the one who had put those pieces together.

He grabbed his laptop and opened it to his project plans. If DiMarco was behind the vandalism, Grayson didn't want to be in business with the guy. But he didn't know for sure DiMarco was. Just because he stood to benefit the most didn't mean there wasn't something else going on—like ecoterrorism or some other angry individual out for revenge that they just hadn't figured out yet.

The sick feeling in his stomach grew. There had always been rumors that DiMarco was shady. Grayson had even questioned including him in the deal originally for that reason, but dismissed it as gossip. But was it really? The old saying, where there's smoke, there's fire... But he didn't want to convict a guy based on gossip. How would he ever know?

God, I could use some wisdom here. How do I convince Cait

that I'm on her side? I want to protect her, not harm her. And what do I do about DiMarco?

He looked at the project again. What if he did it without DiMarco? He tried to look at the project with new eyes. There might be a possibility, but he was too tired to see it. Could he trust God to direct the next step?

Flopping back against the couch, he picked up his phone. He could call DiMarco and see what he wanted. Maybe that would help him figure out what to do.

Darkness had filled the room while Cait laid curled up on her bed, Cam asleep next to her. Her eyes were swollen, and her throat hurt. She flipped on the bedside lamp. She didn't feel like eating anything, but a cup of tea would help. Maybe that and a good book while soaking in the tub would help her feel better. At least take her mind off things. In the morning, she might see things more clearly.

She swung off the bed; Cam didn't stir. She headed downstairs, flipping on lights as she went. She wished it were already summer when the days were longer. The rain made things particularly gloomy.

Downstairs, she made tea in her favorite mug and found the book she'd been reading. Back upstairs in the bathroom, she started the tub. California was under a drought, and she wanted to do her part to not waste water. So while the water took forever to warm up, she had a five-gallon bucket for the water to run into until it warmed. It could go on her garden, though it wouldn't need watering for a while after all the rain today.

She set her mug and book on the antique milking stool next to the tub then headed to her room for her jammies and robe. She was done with this day.

Just as she reentered the bathroom, the lights went off.

Lovely. Now the electrical was out. Could this day get any worse? This was exactly why she had hoped to have the money to fix the electrical before now. Shutting off the water, she pulled her phone out and flipped on the flashlight app. She heard Cam jump off the bed and pad over to her. "Come on, boy. Let's see what's wrong now."

Two steps down the stairs, she heard the back door open and shut. The wind? That didn't make any sense. The hair on the back of her neck stood up. Was it the vandal? Or was there an innocent explanation?

Legs like water, she took the next step down, careful to avoid the creaky spots, straining to hear anything else. Her blood rushed to her head, her pulse so loud in her ears she probably couldn't hear anything.

At the bottom step, Cam let out a soft growl. Was there an animal in the house? Right, an animal that could turn doorknobs. She shone her phone light down the hall and into the living room. Everything looked okay. She needed to check the back door, but she was flat-out afraid. Which was completely ridiculous. Wasn't it? She'd never been afraid in her own home before.

But she'd never been the victim of a series of deliberate attacks either. Should she call the police? But if it was just an animal or the wind, she'd feel stupid.

Embarrassed maybe, but alive. Shoving down her pride, she touched the phone screen, shutting off the flashlight and bringing up the keypad.

With a barking growl, Cam shot off to the kitchen.

"Cam!" She darted after him.

His barking drowned out nearly any other sound, but she heard a muffled curse. She stopped before reaching the kitchen and punched in 911. Backing down the hall, she ran into the living room. She knew this house better than whoever else was in here with her. Right now, darkness was her friend.

Another muffled curse and the squeaky floorboard in the hallway.

She edged toward the dining room, the 911 operator's voice in her ear. "I have an intruder," she whispered, giving her address. Hoping that was good enough, she shoved the phone in her pocket, still on. She would need both hands free.

Another step, plus Cam's barking, let her know the intruder was at the bottom of the stairs. She didn't want him going up there. She tried to make a noise, a shout, but her voice barely squeaked. He probably didn't hear it because he stepped on the bottom tread.

She jumped on the squeaky board just inside the dining room and was rewarded with a footstep in the hall. Forcing her legs to move, she hurried into the dining room and bent down, shoving the plywood off to the side. He had to have heard that.

He did. He was in the living room now, slowly walking toward the dining room.

She backed up to the dining room window. There wasn't much room to escape if this didn't work.

The footsteps stopped.

She needed him to keep moving. "Hey!" Her voice cracked, and she tried again. "What do you want? Who are you?"

The steps moved again, this time with more certainty as they oriented toward her voice.

"Why do you keep doing this to me?" Anger began rising over her fear. "Who do you think you are, trying to ruin my life?"

A slight chuckle then a step and a crack of wood. "Wha—" A muffled thump and a curse as he fell through the hole in the dining room floor.

More energized now, she grabbed the plywood and shoved it back over the hole. That should keep him until the police came. Hopefully, he was afraid of spiders.

Cam stood over the plywood and continued to bark and growl. She'd let him.

"Cait?" Grayson's voice came from the back porch.

She hurried to him, careful to avoid the kitchen island. "I'm here." Pulling the phone out of her pocket, she saw she was still connected. "I have the intruder locked in my root cellar. Please hurry."

"What?" Grayson put his arm around her shoulder and pulled her to him. Grateful, she sank into his embrace.

"Are you in any immediate danger?" the operator asked.

"No, I don't think he can get out. But please hurry."

"Units are on their way. But stay on the line."

"Cait, what's going on? Why are the lights out?"

"I don't know. But I suspect the vandal in my root cellar had something to do with it. Why are you here?"

A thumping noise from the plywood drew their attention.

Grayson snapped on his phone light, and they saw the plywood jump off the floor a few inches with each thump. He ran over and stood on the plywood, keeping it from moving.

"Units are on site," came the voice through the phone Cait had almost forgotten she was holding. "Where in the house are you?"

"In the kitchen. They'll have to come through the back door. I have a friend here too now. He's helping keep the intruder trapped." She didn't want them to think Grayson was the intruder.

The back door burst open. "Police!"

A flashlight shone in her face, and she lifted her hands and pointed to the dining room. "Under there, under the plywood he's standing on."

Grayson lifted his hands and slowly stepped off the plywood.

One officer bent down and slid the plywood away.

Cait took a few steps until she could see the face of the man the police were shining their lights on.

It was the same man she had seen at the farm.

Chapter Ten

Cait tossed her purse and keys on the kitchen counter, smothering a yawn. It had been a long day, and her brain still had a lot to process. The Samashimas had offered to give her the day off, but she knew she'd need to be available to field calls and emails from the media, customers, and vendors.

And she had as soon as the news hit about Greg Connor, the man the police had pulled from her root cellar. But they didn't know much else about him because he wasn't talking. Which didn't give her much to say to anyone who asked.

The good news was her electrical was fine. For now. Connor had just thrown the main power switch at the breaker box.

She grabbed a Diet Coke out of the fridge and hurried upstairs to change into clothes suitable for dirty work. Grayson would be here any minute to help fix the porch stairs. She was grateful for his presence Saturday night while the police and Detective Taylor did their work and asked their questions. Grayson had shared his theory about DiMarco. However, it was just a theory; there was no proof to go on.

They hadn't talked about their fight. She was a little ashamed of herself and still a little leery. He'd come back because he hadn't wanted to leave things between them the way they were. But as it was, they didn't have the time or energy to talk. He'd left after the last officer was gone in the early hours of the morning.

The rumble of the Charger's engine pulling into her driveway let her know Grayson was here. She headed back downstairs and pulled open the back door, grateful that they'd both been able to leave work early to give them extra daylight to work.

He kissed her cheek as he entered. "How was today?"

"Not too bad. I'm tired, took a lot of inquiries, but I didn't have much to tell anyone."

He nodded. "I brought you a surprise." He laughed. "I don't think most women would appreciate it, but I think you will. Come out to the car."

He popped open the trunk and brought out two halogen work lights on tripods, which he began unfolding. "Now we can work as late as we want."

She laughed. "You're amazing. Thank you."

They grabbed tools and the lumber she'd bought and headed out to the front yard. She clipped the leash to Cam then tied it to a long piece of rope tied around the palm tree in her front yard.

They had cleared away the broken boards and were measuring for the footings when her neighbor Mrs. Ballard walked up.

"Seems like you've got a big job there."

"Hi, Mrs. Ballard. Yes, there's a bit of work." Cait stood and took a step toward the sidewalk.

"Quite a to do here the other night. Are you okay?"

She nodded. "I'm fine. The intruder fell through the floor in my dining room, and the police came quickly."

"I hoped so. I was actually out walking because it was the first break in the rain. I saw all the lights in your house flash off and then heard your dog barking nonstop. Something didn't seem right so I called the police."

"Thank you for doing that." Cait paused. "Has Cam's barking bothered you before?"

"Oh, no. I could hardly hear him, and I was standing right here. It was the nonstop nature of the barking combined with the lights going off that made me suspicious."

"Well, thank you again."

Mrs. Ballard squeezed Cait's arm. "I just think it's lovely all the work you've put in on this old house. Glad somebody thought to save it."

Cait smiled. "Thank you. It's a lot of work, as you can see, but I think it's worth it."

"Me too." Mrs. Ballard nodded then continued on her walk.

Cait went back to where Grayson was working. "Getting hungry? I thought I'd have a pizza delivered."

"Sounds good. We won't have to take much of a break."

She placed the order then put her phone on the porch. "I think Mrs. Ballard just proved my point. I knew Cam's barking couldn't be heard enough to bother anyone. So did Greg leave that note as one more way to harass me?"

"We'll never know for sure, but I'd bet yes."

They continued working until the pizza came. Cait grabbed a couple of Diet Cokes and paper plates from inside. They sat on the porch, feet dangling over the missing stair section.

Grayson set his plate down. "I talked to Kyle today—Detective Taylor. He told me Greg Connor made bail at his arraignment today."

She nodded. "He told me that too. They put a personal protection order out so he has to stay away from me. I probably should feel more afraid, but I really don't. I think his scare tactics only worked from the shadows. Now that we know who he is, it doesn't seem like there is much he can do."

"I did some digging on him, none of which will mean

anything in court, but it all bolsters our theory. Connor has worked as a general contractor for DiMarco before. Of course, he's worked for other developers too. But the lawyer representing him today is one DiMarco has on retainer."

He reached for her hand. "I called off the deal with DiMarco today. While I can't prove that he's involved, in my gut I know he is. And I don't want to do business with anyone like that, no matter how lucrative."

"Oh, Grayson." Her heart lurched. "All that work you put into it. It was going to be your next big thing."

"I know. And I still don't know what DiMarco was up to with the text and call Saturday night. He wouldn't answer my calls. But I figure he knew Greg was coming over here to threaten you, and you'd be scared off. I think he took my probing over our lunch as interest in doing some shady work and that text was to see if I would bite."

"But your project ..." The pizza sat hard in her stomach. She wasn't the only one that had suffered because of this mess.

And she owed Grayson an apology for how she acted. She'd responded out of fear, not faith. "Grayson—"

He put his finger over her lips. "Shh. I want to say something. Remember last Christmas when we spent all of those services hanging out when we weren't singing?"

She nodded.

"We made a connection there. I got to know you and wanted to know you more. I had planned to ask you out, but I didn't want to call you out of the blue. Then you were sick and missed a bunch of practices and then I was on vacation. We just kept missing each other. When Bernie said you needed a ride, I jumped at the chance. And he knew I would because he knew I was interested in you."

He took both her hands. "Cait, I want you to know beyond a shadow of a doubt that I like you for who you are. You are the most fascinating, complex, determined woman I know. And that doesn't scare me. It makes me want to know more."

Her heart clogged her throat and tears stung her eyes. Why had she ever doubted him? The memories from the past were powerful, but they needed to be put to rest.

"Grayson, I'm so sor—" Her words were cut off as he claimed her lips. Her hands went around his neck, clinging to him.

So what if the neighbors could see?

Epilogue

Cait wiped her forehead with the back of her hand. Her hair was piled up high to get it off her neck, but she was still hot. The kitchen was steamy with pots of boiling water and strawberry jam cooking on the stove.

Grayson kissed her neck.

"Grayson!" She laughed. "Pay attention to the jam. You have to keep stirring it."

He went back to his assigned task. "So this is your grandma's recipe."

"Yep. I can't tell you how many jars I've made over the years. But it's the best. Tastes like fresh strawberries."

"I can't wait to try it. So how did your interview go with Monica West?"

Grayson had come up with a great idea. Greg Connor was only being charged with vandalism and likely would get off with just a fine. Since everything they had on DiMarco was conjecture, why not beat him to the punch? Monica West was more than willing to do a piece on the state of farming in Orange County and how development threatened it. The paper even printed a map showing the land owners around the farm. DiMarco's name was quite evident. If anything else happened, he'd have some explaining to do.

"She's quite the character. She loved the idea and kept digging and coming up with ideas. I think the best thing we could have done was sic her on DiMarco. He won't be able to make a move without her knowing it."

She dropped the paring knife she had been using to cut strawberries and ran her hands under the faucet. They were faintly pink from all the juice. "How did your client presentation go?"

"Better than I could have hoped. The new project, revamped without DiMarco, actually makes a lot more sense. I couldn't see it before when I assumed he had to be in the picture. But with him out of it, it's a much better situation. Everyone got on board, and we start moving forward next week."

Contentment warmed her inside like melted butter.

As soon as the jam was ready, they poured it into jars, capped them, and set them to boil.

After they got all the jars filled, boiled, and cooling, they headed out to the front porch with glasses of iced tea.

She looked around the front porch. "I need some furniture out here. There's no good place to sit."

"We can sit on these lovely front porch steps." He moved to sit down, and she joined him.

She grinned. "They are lovely, aren't they? Like someone spent a few late nights to make them look right and beat the deadline." She nudged his shoulder.

He put down his glass. "And I'm willing to go to a lot more trouble for you." He reached behind and pulled out a small gift bag and handed it to her.

She raised her eyebrows as she took it.

"Just look inside."

Reaching in, she pulled out tissue paper. As she unwrapped it, a long, fine chain fell out. On the chain was an old fashioned key with PROMISE stamped on it. Next to it hung a small charm in the shape of a hammer.

"Oh, Grayson. It's perfect."

He took the chain and hung it over her head. "It's just the first of many. I promise." He took her face in his hands and kissed her long and deeply.

Who cared if the neighbors saw?

Are you curious about what happens next?

What will Greg Connor and Tony DiMarco get up to next? What's reporter Monica West's next investigative piece?

And what about handsome Detective Kyle Taylor? What's in store for him?

Find out by signing up for my latest news and updates at www.jlcrosswhite.com/landing-page and you'll get the Hometown Heroes short story, "Never Met a Stranger" as well as the stand-alone contemporary novella, *The Inn at Cherry Blossom Lane.*

My bimonthly updates include upcoming books written by me (Scott and Melissa's story, S*pecial Assignment: Hometown Heroes book 3,* will release in summer 2019 and you'll be the first to know) and other authors you will enjoy, information on all my latest releases, sneak peeks of yet-to-be-released chap-ters, and exclusive giveaways. Your email address will never be shared, and you can unsubscribe at any time.

If you enjoyed this book, please consider leaving a review. Reviews can be as simple as "I couldn't put it down. I can't wait for the next one" and help raise the author's visibility and lets other readers find her.

Keep reading for a sneak peak of *Protective Custody: Hometown Heroes book 1*

ACKNOWLEDGMENTS

This book would not be possible without my craft partners, Diana Brandmeyer and Liz Tolsma. Many thanks to my beta reader, Danielle Reid, and proofreader, Sara Benner. And to my family for putting up with my time at the computer and time with my head in the clouds living in my characters' world. But most of all, to my Lord Jesus Christ, who makes all of this possible.

Author's Note

Laguna Vista isn't a real town, but it's based on the area of Orange County that I lived in for twelve years. As with many stories, a confluence of ideas came together that I wanted to explore. Not to mention it's a beautiful location with the ocean to the west and foothills and mountains to the east and the austere-but-beautiful desert within driving distance.

The area has an interesting juxtaposition of wealth and conservatism. Christianity is both embraced and challenged in this area. It's home to Rick Warren's Saddleback Church, a church I attended and served at. One of the questions I struggled with while living there was how does someone live an authentic Christian life while daily challenged with the trappings of an affluent lifestyle? Cars, houses, jewelry, beauty all add up to one thing in Orange County: image. It's the most valuable commodity.

So how does a Christian reconcile being made in the image of God with society's image? Ultimately, all the characters in the book must deal with this question on their faith journey. Each of them has their own unique image, yet all are made in the image of God. I hope that is one thing you will take away from reading *Promise Me* and that you will be encouraged to reflect on how uniquely you are made in the image of God.

About Me

My favorite thing is discovering how much there is to love about America the Beautiful and the great outdoors. I'm an Amazon bestselling author, a mom to two navigating the young adult years while battling my daughter's juvenile arthritis, exploring the delights of my son's autism, and keeping gluten free. A California native who's spent significant time in the Midwest, I'm thrilled to be back in the Golden State. Follow me on social media to see all my adventures and how I get inspired for my books!

www.JLCrosswhite.com
Twitter: @jenlcross
Facebook: Author Jennifer Crosswhite
Instagram: jencrosswhite
Pinterest: Author Jennifer Crosswhite

Sneak Peek Protective Custody Hometown Heroes book 1.

Not spending money on Bernie's caffeine addiction was almost as good as shooting fifty free throws without missing. Detective Kyle Taylor glanced at his watch as he drove his unmarked Crown Vic back to the station. He was going to make it on time, despite covering a shift for Mark, whose wife just had a baby. And that meant Starbucks would be Bernie's treat.

The radio crackled, the constant background music to his life. "...stolen white Lexus SUV. Suspects are four males, Caucasian, heading northbound on El Toro. Passing Jeronimo."

His attention ratcheted up, along with his pulse. That was three-K twelve, Jeff Griffin. A rookie on his first pursuit. His gut tightened. They were headed his way. Detectives didn't usually get involved in pursuits. But Griffin made this different. Kyle had been his training officer and didn't want to think about what would happen if he hadn't trained Griffin well enough.

He hit the lights and sirens on his unmarked cruiser, making it marginally more visible, then snatched the dashboard mic. "David fifty-seven to three King twelve, moving to intercept from Trabuco and El Toro."

As he turned the corner on El Toro, he spotted the pursuit in his rearview mirror. They were moving to a section four lanes wide and, on a Sunday morning, not too busy.

The lieutenant's voice snapped over the radio. "All units be advised David fifty-seven has the handle on this pursuit."

Kyle groaned. Not only was he going to be late, he would miss the early service completely. Which meant he'd be getting Bernie a Caffe Mocha. Venti or grande? He could never remember what the sizes meant. None of that would matter if he screwed this up. The lieutenant was like his dad. He expected results, not excuses. And a good outcome of this pursuit was all that mattered.

The Lexus SUV in his rearview mirror grew big in a hurry. Kyle forced himself to scan the street in front of him, to avoid tunnel vision on his mirror. "Pursuit is headed toward Portola Parkway. Any units available to intercept, please respond." He moved across the lanes, trying to keep the suspect behind him.

"Three King thirty-two is responding. I'm headed up Lake Forest. ETA two minutes."

"Three King thirty-five responding, currently at Los Alisos and Santa Margarita Parkway."

Mission Viejo, huh? Patino must have been at that hamburger and donut shop—weird combo, but Patino swore by it. At times Kyle wished he could let things roll off his back the way Patino did. But then that's why Kyle had made detective and Patino hadn't. Yet.

A glance at his speedometer. As he pushed the gas pedal down, the needle crept up.

The Lexus jerked into the oncoming lane.

Kyle scanned the road ahead. Around the curve, a delivery truck barreled down on them. He winced. *Lord, don't let anyone get hurt.*

Checking the rearview mirror, he saw the suspect cut in front of the truck. With a screech of brakes, smoke billowed out behind the truck. Narrowly missing the truck, the Lexus swerved off-road, kicking up dust. Back on the pavement now, he closed in on Portola.

Kyle punched the accelerator. He had to reach the intersection ahead of the suspect. Gauging the distance, he slammed on the brakes. His car slid across the center of the intersection.

The SUV still bore down on Kyle.

He swiped the back of his hand across his forehead. Which way would the suspect go? He scanned the area trying to predict.

Tires skidding and rear end fishtailing—coming within inches of sideswiping Kyle's cruiser—the Lexus swerved, cut the corner, jumped the curb, and headed into the hills.

Kyle floored it, squealing the tires as he willed the big V8 engine to race from a near standstill to now playing catch-up.

His pulse throbbed in his neck. Someone was going to get hurt. So far he had a clean jacket on pursuits, no write ups in his file. But if something went bad, no matter what, Kyle's career was on the line.

There was an elementary school coming up. He tightened his grip on the steering wheel. Kyle closed in as they crested the hill. His breaths came closer together.

They'd soon be out of Laguna Vista city limits. Over the radio, Griffin requested assistance from the sheriff's department.

The Lexus accelerated down the hill, out of the residential area.

He blew a sigh of relief. They had a real shot at ending this now. Glenn Ranch looped around and dead-ended back at El Toro. They had the suspect trapped. Unless he went into the canyons.

The SUV shrieked left onto El Toro and headed back into the hills, destined for either Live Oak or Silverado Canyon.

Kyle followed, all three squad cars now trailing him. They approached Live Oak Canyon at nearly seventy miles an hour. He hoped the suspect wouldn't try to make the cutoff. It was a sharp turn and Cook's Corner, a local biker hangout shack, sat close to the road. He could just see the SUV missing the turn and plowing into the dirt lot full of Harleys.

They passed Live Oak. Another relief.

El Toro Road became Santiago Canyon. Not as twisty as Live Oak, but still plenty of curves. Not many places to turn off, either, other than some private and fire roads. With the sheriff's department coming from the other direction, they should have the suspect trapped soon.

Taillights strobed. Kyle slammed his foot on the brake.

The suspect's car slung onto a dirt road. Kyle followed, the kicked-up dust obscuring his vision. He bounced over the rough terrain, brush scraping the sides of his cruiser. His unit had beefed up suspension, but it wasn't an SUV.

The Lexus attempted a hairpin switchback. Too fast. The back end slid out. It tilted up on two wheels, hovered, then slammed on its side.

Kyle's unit shuddered to a stop. He called for EMS, throwing the mic on the seat as he jumped out. Others pulled in behind.

Drawing his gun, he covered the vehicle, waiting for backup. Dust settled around it, eerily silent. He took a deep breath, trying to slow the adrenaline racing through his veins.

The airbags had deployed, blocking the side windows, but the back liftgate window revealed no movement. A groan came from inside.

It hadn't ended safely for these guys. A twinge ricocheted in Kyle's chest. He didn't like people getting hurt. It was a big part of his job to prevent that. But these guys made their own consequences when they decided to steal a car.

Griffin ran up behind him, his gun also covering the SUV. Lopez and Patino followed.

"Anybody hurt?" Lopez's voice came from behind Kyle.

"Can't tell." Kyle studied the vehicle then squatted, peering through the liftgate window. Looked like two in front, two in back. Tinted windows made it hard to see, especially in the shadows. "Can you hear me in there?"

"Uh, yeah. I think my arm's broken." A young voice, like a teenage boy's.

"Okay, we've got an ambulance on the way. Who else is in there?"

"Hey, Alex. You awake, man? Alex? Cole?"

Kyle heard the panic in the voice.

"I can't get any of them to answer me." Tears now too. "Trevor's next to me, and he's got blood coming out of his head."

Griffin thumbed his shoulder-mounted radio requesting an ETA for the ambulance. The kids were scared now, but most of the time it didn't stick.

"Three king twelve, that's fifteen plus."

He looked up and holstered his gun. "Let's see what we can do."

Patino nodded and pulled out his baton.

Kyle turned to the window again. "We're going to break out this back window so we can help you. I'll need you to cover your face. What's your name?"

"Justin. Justin Foster."

Kyle froze. Justin?

On a hill overlooking the scene of the wrecked SUV, Bull studied the activity through his binoculars. Hiding between two boulders, sand digging into his elbows, Bull yanked the binoculars from his eyes, swearing. Rage pumped up the veins in his arms, fisting his hands. He had to punch something, like Alex's face.

He wanted that SUV, and the quick cash it would bring. It was so simple, but Pretty Boy managed to screw it up.

One minute farther on the dirt road and the cops would have been too close. Way too close. Bull would have lost more than the SUV. A lot more.

Hearing the *thwap thwap thwap* of the sheriff's helicopter, he double-checked his cover, glad he'd worn desert camos. With the uniforms and what looked like a plainclothes guy down there, that chopper wouldn't hang around long. He and his boys were safe. For now.

But Alex? That was a whole other deal. Bull didn't put up with stupidity.

Too bad.

He'd had high hopes for that boy. Now he'd need a replacement.

HEATHER MCALISTAIR CROSSED THE STAGE and stepped onto the risers under the scorching lights. Looking out over the church congregation, she was thankful this was the last of three services. The back of her throat tickled. She attempted to cough discreetly. It didn't help. She swallowed. And chewed on the side of her tongue. None of her normal tricks were working. She needed something to drink. Desperately. Why hadn't she grabbed a bottle of water before she left this morning? Because she was running late as usual.

"You okay?" Bernie nudged her shoulder.

His curly hair was sticking up from running his hands through it. She never could decide if his plastic-rimmed glasses were nerdy or trendy. Most likely he didn't care. For all his life-of-the-party personality, he was pretty aware—for a guy.

"I've got something in my throat and no water."

"Here." He handed her a cough drop. "Not as good as water but better than nothing."

"Thanks." She popped it in her mouth, scanning the congregation while the rest of the choir filed in.

A few people stood in the back of the worship center. One man in particular caught her attention. He leaned against the wall holding two coffee cups. Why did he look familiar? She didn't know why. He smiled at her.

She slid her gaze away and fiddled with one of her bracelets. This was the worst part, everyone watching before she could lose herself in the music and forget the audience. She smiled and hoped it looked genuine.

Absently, she scanned the rest of the congregation, looking for familiar faces. She spotted a few and smiled.

She had moved on before her brain registered a face.

A sharp intake of breath and the cough drop slid partway down her throat and stuck. She coughed to dislodge it. Her eyes watered. She blinked rapidly and took a breath.

Afraid of what she might have seen, she couldn't bring herself to look again. Surely her mind was playing tricks on her. He wasn't here. He was in New York.

Wasn't he?

Working to keep her expression neutral, she snuck a glance. Third row, aisle seat.

Yep, he was there.

Quinn.

Grinning up at her.

Her stomach lurched, and she was afraid she was going to be sick. Why was he here?

A million questions raced through her mind. But someone stepped into her field of view. Ryan Bradley, their worship leader, raised his eyebrows at her.

She stepped forward to pick up the mic. She pressed her lips together and forced down the twitches in her stomach. If she got nervous, her voice would tighten and shake, and she'd sound terrible. She couldn't deal with Quinn now. Forcibly, she pushed him out of her mind.

Closing her eyes, she focused on the words of the song. Audience of One, right? She wasn't doing this for Quinn or anyone else out there.

Before she brought the mic up, she tried to hum the note she needed. But nothing happened. Her voice locked up. Panic rose from her diaphragm threatening to drown her. Disaster stared at her, wearing Quinn's face.

She glanced over her shoulder, hoping to catch Ryan's eye, to warn him or something. He was focused on the choir. She took a step back, wanting to rush back and blend into the choir.

It was too late. Ryan turned and pointed at her.

The drummer counted out the beat.

She had to sing the first word before the band played the note. She had to be right on.

Everyone was waiting on her.

She swallowed, trying to loosen the knot. Closing her eyes and imagining the music in her mind, she let her breath out and back in.

And sang. The first line. Right on.

She opened her eyes.

The room faded away, and Heather was only aware of the music and voices flowing around her. Her voice seemed to be singing on its own, without any direction from her.

On the chorus, the choir and congregation joined in. Heather lowered the mic and stepped back into the safety of the choir, legs barely holding her.

As one of the pastors gave the announcements, Heather looked to the man in the back. He gave her a thumbs-up and a smile that caused a flicker of warmth—it fought against the panic that filled her heart.

Kyle eased out of the worship center and into the courtyard as the choir left the stage. He plopped down on the wide edge of a concrete planter, setting the coffee cups next to him, waiting for Bernie to come out. As people passed him, meandering into church, he let himself relax, still trying to shake the dregs of the adrenaline rush from the car chase. Loudspeakers broadcast the announcements so those coming in late or sitting outside wouldn't miss anything. He'd have to get the sermon online later.

The woman singing had a beautiful voice. There was something to it that made him believe what she was singing. He enjoyed watching her too, with her soft brown eyes and light brown hair, cut just below her chin but with something done to it so it didn't quite look like a basic cut. He guessed her height to be about five seven, slender build. Classic, understated beauty that was a perfect backdrop for her fun sense of fashion. He didn't know much about that, but her long, multicolored print skirt and about twenty bracelets on her arms revealed a unique sense of style.

And her playing with those same bracelets revealed her nervousness. Interesting. He hadn't noticed that before. Something had disturbed her. More than that, at one point she looked downright panicked. His radar for something wrong pinged.

Maybe he should head back to the green room to find Bernie. He'd deliver the coffee and maybe even run into her. Figure out what had spooked her. He wasn't going to sort out if it was personal or professional interest.

It'd been an adventurous morning already. After the car chase, he had to call Justin's mom, Claire, and break the news to her. Kyle had taught Justin's fifth grade Sunday school class. He was about the last kid Kyle expected to pull out of that wrecked SUV. Made him wonder how many of the lessons had stuck with the kids.

Claire came to the station to pick up Justin dressed like she was ready to go to Fashion Island or South Coast Plaza instead of church. How she hadn't noticed Justin was missing was something he didn't understand, but Kyle hadn't been in touch with the Fosters much the last few years.

She'd ranted at the station about how Justin's father, who lived in New York, was already catching a flight to Orange County and was not pleased. He'd felt helpless, as usual, in the face of women's emotions.

"But then, when is he ever pleased about anything involving his son?" She waved her hand as if that wiped the thought away. Her tone softened. "Anyway, if Justin was trying to get his dad's attention, he got it. Thanks for all you've done. I know it could have been much worse for him."

He'd talked to Claire a bit longer, trying to figure out how to get Justin involved with some kids who would be a better influence on him. He refused to go to the church youth group, saying all the kids were losers. But hanging around Alex and his friends wasn't a good move either. Just because this time the car they took happened to belong to Alex's stepmom didn't mean that next one wouldn't really be stolen. Justin was lucky he only suffered a sprained shoulder, but next time could be worse.

And there would be a next time. Kyle had been at this job long enough to know that. Justin's dad, living way across the country, didn't have time for him. His mom was frustrated and didn't have any control over him. She was doing her best, but she needed more help than she was getting. Kyle mentally scrolled through a list of people he could call. How hard was it to point a teenager in the right direction?

He could spend some time with the kid. Would Justin be willing to get up early enough on a Saturday to hit the waves? He'd never gone surfing with someone he'd arrested.

He hopped off the planter and grabbed the coffees. He was going to hunt down Bernie. And maybe that pretty lady too.

Something grabbed Heather's shoulder. She jumped, her pulse rocketing into the blue Southern California sky, and spun around.

Bernie.

She let out a breath and hoped he didn't notice.

"You okay? You look a little pale."

"I'm fine. It was hot up there. Kind of got to me." She spotted her purse on a chair in the green room. Grabbing it, she slung it over her shoulder. She had to get out of here before Quinn showed up. It would be like him to duck out of church early to try to catch her. She didn't want to talk to him, see him, or have anything to do with him again. Ever.

"A bunch of us from my small group are going to lunch. Join us?"

"Well—"

"Come on, Heather. It'll be good for you."

Heather let him propel her out the door. Using Bernie as a shield against Quinn was cowardly, especially since she didn't feel in the mood to go to lunch. Her small talk game—never very good to begin with—would be lousy today, and she'd end up sounding stupid. Plus, she liked Bernie, but not in *that* way, and she didn't want him to get any ideas. This was not a good idea, but she couldn't figure out how to tell him no.

"Hey, Kyle." Bernie came to a stop.

Heather licked her suddenly dry lips. A tall man with close-cut sandy blond hair handed a Starbucks cup to Bernie. The same man who'd been standing in the back of the church. The scent of chocolate-laced coffee drifted to her. Good looking, he nicely filled out his polo shirt. She didn't dare look for a ring; she'd get caught for sure and wouldn't that just be humiliating? Instead she searched out his eyes. They were gray, the color of the ocean on a cloudy day.

"Hey, Bernie. You guys sounded great up there."

"Oh, you actually caught some of the service?" Bernie turned to look at Heather, then back at Kyle. "Kyle, do you know Heather?" He took a sip from his cup.

Kyle extended his hand. "No, I haven't had the pleasure, but I know your face from your singing in the choir. I'm Kyle Taylor." His gaze seemed a touch too intense, almost searching, like he'd asked a question she hadn't heard.

"Heather McAlistair." She shook his hand. Warm, large, a little rough with calluses. She couldn't think of a thing to say, as usual. "Nice to meet you." Her tongue stuck like it was glued to the roof of her mouth.

"I covered for Mark last night and had a pursuit this

morning. But, as you can see"—he gestured to the Starbucks cup—"I made good on our deal. And I'm planning to go to lunch before I go home and crash. Heather, are you joining us?"

"Yes, she is." Bernie took her arm and started maneuvering her toward the parking lot.

Out of the corner of her eye, she saw Quinn headed straight toward her. She froze. Her breath caught, her heart picked up tempo. It *was* him. Part of her still hadn't been sure, had hoped she'd imagined him.

But there he was grinning at her, sun glinting off his dark, wavy hair, that same spring in his step, like everything in his life was absolutely fantastic.

"Heather!" He wrapped her in a bear hug, trapping her arms at her side, sliding her purse off her shoulder. He stepped back, still grasping her shoulders. "How are you? You look fantastic. And you sounded terrific as always."

And Quinn was still overwhelming. She took a step back, thankful for Bernie's presence and embarrassed by Kyle's. "Fine." She was amazed her voice worked, even sounded somewhat normal.

Kyle stepped forward and introduced himself, forcing Quinn to let go of Heather. She gave him a grateful smile. He smiled back, and her stomach did a funny little jump.

Quinn turned back to her. "Heather, I know it's last minute and you probably already have plans, but I was hoping I could talk you into having lunch with me."

"I have plans." At that moment, she was more than grateful for Bernie's invitation to lunch. No way did she want to go anywhere with Quinn. She couldn't deal with his persistence today.

Quinn's 200-watt smiled dimmed a bit. "Sure. I understand."

What? No argument? He wasn't trying to invite himself along? "I thought you were in New York." She couldn't resist. Her curiosity got the better of her.

"I still am. I'm just out here visiting my folks. Miss this gorgeous California weather."

"I see." She shifted her weight, looking around for a way out.

Kyle's gaze flicked from her to Bernie to Quinn. Was it her imagination or did his eyebrows raise a bit? She wanted to get out of here, even if her escape route involved going to lunch with people she didn't know.

"Okay, well, I'd better get going." Quinn pulled keys out of his pocket. "Heather, I'll call you tomorrow. Still have the same number?"

She nodded reflexively. She did not want Quinn calling her. But she *really* didn't want to make a scene in front of Kyle and Bernie. What kind of impression must she be making on Kyle? Couldn't she ever do anything the normal way?

"Nice to meet you all." Quinn gave a small wave then turned and left.

She couldn't believe he left without putting up more of a fuss, but she wasn't going to complain. Maybe Quinn had changed. Heather stifled a sigh of relief. She was exhausted and it was still morning. She should excuse herself from lunch. She was too flustered, and that increased her foot-to-mouth ratio. And what if Quinn hadn't given up? What if he was waiting to ambush them at a restaurant?

On the other hand, Kyle and Bernie had been helpful in shielding her from Quinn. Though that might get old for them if Quinn was persistent. Neither of them knew what Quinn did last year. She didn't want a repeat.

"We can take my truck." Kyle pulled keys from his pocket and gestured to the parking lot as they started walking.

"Sounds good," Bernie said. "I'd be too nervous to drive with a cop in my car anyway."

Kyle was a cop? Heather glanced at him out of the corner of her eye. It fit.

Kyle clapped Bernie on the shoulder. "I'd go easy on you."

They stepped out of the intermittent shade of the trees and buildings and onto the warm asphalt. The marine layer of low, thick clouds present this morning had burned off, leaving a sapphire blue sky, the hallmark of a typically beautiful Southern California day. She wished she could enjoy it.

At the restaurant, Kyle introduced her around. One of the women, Melissa, flipped her thick chestnut hair over her shoulder, her dark-eyed gaze holding Heather's. Melissa was confident with a slightly exotic beauty. Heather hadn't looked in the mirror, but she was willing to bet her makeup had all but melted off under the stage lights. She resisted the urge to blot her face with her napkin.

Heather glanced around at the other diners before she realized she was looking for Quinn. With his sell-ice-to-an-Eskimo skills, he would get himself invited to sit with these unsuspecting people or at the very least sit across the room where she couldn't miss his presence.

Kyle pulled out the chair next to Melissa, holding it for Heather to slide into. Then he took the seat next to her at the head of the table. That was nice. It'd been a long time since anyone had been so gentlemanly toward her. She took a deep breath to head off a yawn. The adrenaline of the morning was draining off. Quinn hadn't shown up, so maybe she could relax. Now as long as she didn't do anything stupid, maybe she could enjoy Kyle's company.

Melissa was talking to the person on the other side of her and Heather didn't understand the context of the conversation. Something about last summer. But it triggered a thought in Heather's mind, and she studied Melissa while she wasn't watching. Could she be…?

Quinn had dated a Melissa before Heather. Heather had never met her but she'd seen pictures. This Melissa could be the same one. Hard to tell just from pictures. A weird feeling slithered into her stomach. Was this some sort of elaborate set up by Quinn? She surveyed the restaurant more thoroughly.

"Tired?" Kyle's breath brushed her ear, sending shivers down her spine.

"A little," she said, surprised at how perceptive he was. She dropped the thoughts of Melissa with Quinn and turned her attention to Kyle. "My Jitter Bug house special wore off about an hour ago."

"What time did you get to church this morning?"

"Seven."

He winced. "That's early for a Sunday."

"Yes, it is. I'm not sure I've recovered from the Easter marathon last month."

Bernie leaned forward. "Aw, come on, Heather. You'd sing every Sunday if you could."

A smile escaped. "Probably. But ten Easter services were too much even for me."

"The joys of attending a big church."

Bernie brought the discussion around to this morning's sermon, recapping it for Kyle's benefit, he said with a wink.

Heather's gaze strayed to the window and the tropical landscaping brushing against the glass. A car drove by, the sun reflecting off its glass, hiding the driver from her. It was a classic Jaguar, like the one Quinn used to drive. Her pulse notched up as she tried to see where it went. A pause dropped into the conversation, and all eyes seemed to be on her. She tried to remember the subject. Ah, the sermon.

"I'm always amazed at the things people go through that bring them to Christ." That was a safe comment. The speaker today had talked about how the collapse of his business and marriage brought him to Christ and eventually led him to start a ministry in Mexico. She shook her head. "I don't know what I'd have done if I had to go through all that pain and loss."

She snuck a look out the window. The Jaguar was gone. Besides, he'd have his car with him in New York, wouldn't he? Probably wasn't even Quinn.

Bernie leaned his elbows on the table. "Anybody ever gotten up and given their testimony?"

She'd rather die than get up and talk in front of a group, especially about her spiritual life even though she'd been a Christian her whole life. Yeah, she was a real incorrigible six-year-old. Once she threw a temper tantrum when she had to tie her own shoes before Jesus saved her from a life of anger management classes.

Even talking to others about her work made her cringe. On Friday, she got an email asking her to speak to a group of high school girls about her work at the magazine. She responded, "No thank you." Even if speaking in front of a group didn't terrify her, she didn't have anything worthwhile to say. The kids would find her boring and they'd get restless. It would be just an embarrassing mess like the first—and last—time she spoke in front of a group.

Head shakes and a smattering of "not me" rippled around the table like the Wave at Angel Stadium. Until it got to Melissa. Of course, she had given her testimony in front of a crowd. More than once.

The waitress handed Heather a much-desired glass of iced tea. She sipped the cold liquid, soothing her parched throat. Ah, finally. She closed her eyes, rolling her eyeballs against her lids, trying to moisten them. Something to drink, a guy who knew how to be a gentleman, and no Quinn. Going to lunch might have been a good decision.

Even if it had been made for her.

Voices carried from behind her as the hostess seated another party near them. One voice—male—rose above the rest. Heather jerked around expecting to see Quinn's face.

Her elbow hit something cold. Her glass of iced tea. Sending it sprawling across the table.

"Oh! I'm so sorry!" She jumped up and threw her napkin on the spreading puddle, trying to stop it.

Kyle grabbed her glass, set it upright, and added his napkin to her efforts.

The hostess hurried over with a wad of napkins. "Here. You might need these."

"Thanks." Kyle responded before Heather could. He grinned at Heather. "No worries. We've got it under control, and no one got doused."

She was such an idiot. She couldn't even look at him. Quinn managed to ruin this lunch without even being here.

Heather just wanted to get home. It was only early afternoon, but she was exhausted from emotions that ran the gamut. Kyle drove her and Bernie back to the church, pulling up next to the only two cars left in the lot.

Bernie hopped out and opened Heather's door, but Kyle got out too.

"This your Miata?" He nodded to the sporty, forest green convertible.

"Yes. It's my baby."

"Nice." Kyle strolled around her car, checking it out.

"I like it." She smiled, but it faded quickly. Under the windshield wiper, a folded piece of paper fluttered. The edge lifted to reveal a masculine scrawl. She reached back to the truck for balance.

Kyle had stopped next to the driver's door and started to grab the paper then stopped. "Someone left you a note." Something odd crept into his voice.

Steadying herself, she walked over to the car. She hesitated, and then reached for the note.

Kyle halted her with a touch to the back of her hand. "Do you know who left it?"

"I think so." She hoped Kyle would leave it at that. She didn't want to talk about Quinn.

He moved his hand.

She lifted the wiper and grabbed the scrap. Flicking it open, she scanned it, rolled her eyes then crumpled it.

"Bad news?" Kyle stood just behind her. Surprisingly, it was comforting, not oppressive.

"No, annoying. Like the person who left it." She clicked on her key fob to disarm the alarm and unlock the door. He took a step and opened her door for her.

"Thanks." She slid in, tossing her purse and the crumpled note on the passenger seat.

He reached for his wallet and pulled out a business card. He handed it to her. "If someone's bothering you, don't be afraid to let me know."

She took it, their fingers briefly brushing. "Thanks. It's nothing, though." She hoped.

He hesitated, looking like he wanted to say more, but didn't.

Bernie opened the door to his Honda, leaning on the door, but didn't get in. He leaned down to look in her window. "Thanks for coming with us, Heather."

"Thanks for inviting me." She glanced up at Kyle. "I had a good time." And she had. Until now. Leave it to Quinn to ruin things.

"My pleasure," he said. "We'll see you Friday."

Friday night Bible study. Something they all had managed to talk her into at lunch. "Looking forward to it. Bye, Bernie." Kyle closed the door for her. She started the car, flipped on the AC, and slowly backed out, waving as she pulled away.

What was she going to do about Quinn?

Sign up for my latest updates at www.JLCrosswhite.com/landing-page and be the first to know when *Special Assignment: Hometown Heroes book 3* is releasing.

Books by JL Crosswhite

Romantic Suspense
The Hometown Heroes Series

Promise Me

Cait can't catch a break. What she witnessed could cost her job and her beloved farmhouse. Will Greyson help her or only make things worse?

Protective Custody

She's a key witness in a crime shaking the roots of the town's power brokers. He's protecting a woman he'll risk everything for. Doing the right thing may cost her everything. Including her life.

Flash Point

She's a directionally-challenged architect who stumbled on a crime that could destroy her life's work. He's a firefighter protecting his hometown… and the woman he loves.

Special Assignment

A brain-injured Navy pilot must work with the woman in charge of the program he blames for his injury. As they both grasp to save their careers, will their growing attraction hinder them as they attempt solve the mystery of who's really at fault before someone else dies?

Books by Jennifer Crosswhite

Contemporary Romance

The Inn at Cherry Blossom Lane

Can the summer magic of Lake Michigan bring first loves back together? Or will the secret they discover threaten everything they love?

Historical Romance
The Route Home Series

Be Mine

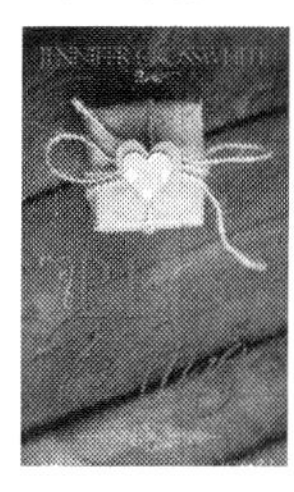

A woman searching for independence. A man searching for education. Can a simple thank you note turn into something more?

Coming Home

He was why she left. Now she's falling for him. Can a woman who turned her back on her hometown come home to find justice for her brother without falling in love with his best friend?

The Road Home

He is a stagecoach driver just trying to do his job. She is returning to her suitor only to find he has died. When a stack of stolen money shows up in her bag, she thinks the past she has desperately tried to hide has come back to haunt her.

66511056R00071

Made in the USA
Middletown, DE
10 September 2019